DAWN RAID

BY PAULINE VAELUAGA SMITH

ILLUSTRATED BY MAT HUNKIN

LQ
LEVINE QUERIDO

MONTCLAIR | AMSTERDAM | NEW YORK

This is an Arthur A. Levine book
Published by Levine Querido

LQ
LEVINE QUERIDO

www.levinequerido.com ✦ info@levinequerido.com
Levine Querido is distributed by Chronicle Books LLC
Text copyright © 2018 by Pauline Vaeluaga Smith
Illustrations copyright © 2021 by Mat Hunkin
Originally published in New Zealand by Scholastic New Zealand
Library of Congress Control Number: 2020937503
ISBN 978-1-64614-041-1
Printed and bound in China

Published March 2021
First Printing

For my parents,
Fou Liki Vaeluaga (Fred) and Raylene
Dawn Ballantyne (née Patterson);
the kids who shared the family nest:
Sandy (Sandra Joy Borland), Rick
(Ricky John Vaeluaga), Dazz
(Darren Fou Vaeluaga);
and Kaye Thorpe who
shared a different nest

This book belongs to:

Sofia Christina Savea
57 Bedford Street
Cannons Creek
Porirua East
Wellington
North Island
New Zealand
♡

SUNDAY, 20 June 1976

Dear Diary,

I can't believe the first McDonald's in the WHOLE country is here—in Porirua!—at the shopping centre in Cobham Court.

They had all sorts of problems with the date for the official opening though. Dad said it was because of "red tape" and had to do with them putting in the wrong benches or something. So it just had its opening ceremony last Saturday, and Mum said when she drove past, there were people lined up out the door and down the footpath! They had to lock the doors and only let more people in when others left.

There was a band playing and Ronald McDonald arrived in a helicopter. The newspaper said when Ronald got out of the helicopter, he went to put up an umbrella, and the helicopter blades sucked it up out of his hands and smashed it into pieces! I bet Ronald got a fright!

Lenny's already been to McDonald's and said he waited for 40 minutes <u>just to order</u>. But, he said it was <u>so</u> worth it. They call the chips "fries" like they do in America. I love it.

They're really, really thin and crunchy and Lenny said he would definitely line up for those again. He said the burger was amazing, with pickle or something like that in it, and they have ketchup instead of tomato sauce. I'd line up for 40 minutes for a taste.

Lenny is so lucky he has a milk run so he can buy his own stuff. Far out!!! If I had a milk run I'd spend all of my first pay on Milkybars and Big Charlie bubblegum. I'd hide them under my bed and eat them at night. I wonder how much Lenny gets paid and how many Milkybars and Big Charlies it would buy.

Anyway, as a special birthday treat, Dad *was* going to take me there for tea today, but sadly, there'll be no McDonald's for me. Those bratty little brothers of mine ruined it. Stinky little scuzz buckets! Mum's still at the hospital with Tavita, Ethan's in his room crying, and their friend Archie got sent home. I think Archie was crying too. Ethan is really scared he'll get a hiding. I hope he does—with Dad's belt!

No, I don't really . . . well, I kinda do. But . . . man, I'm still so mad at them for ruining my special tea with Dad. Oh! I think I can hear the car, Mum's back with Tavita. I'm going to see what happened . . .

Back now.

Everything's okay. Tavita has a small bandage on his head, right beside his eye, and a plaster on his knee. Mum said the doctor gave him a telling-off for being so silly. She thought Tavita deserved it, but Mum thought because he was already upset, it probably wasn't necessary. Dad thought Mum should have taken Ethan and Archie to the hospital as well so the doctor could give them a telling-off too. Dad said, "One kid—one brain, two kids—half a brain, three kids—NO BRAIN AT ALL." I laughed, Tavita cried, Mum groaned, and Dad told us kids to go to bed.

I agree with Dad about the "no brains" though. Those stupid boys were playing darts, taking turns holding the dartboard for each other. It was all fun and games until Tavita was holding the board. Archie tried to be clever and threw all three darts at once. When Mum raced in to see what all the shouting was about, she thought the dart was sticking out of Tavita's EYE (ewww). She got all wobbly on her feet and yelled at Archie to go get his mum. Archie's mum came and pulled the dart out, then Mum rushed Tavita to the hospital. Man, boys are stupid! Why didn't they just climb a tree or something? Mum said the worst part for Tavita was getting an injection for "tech mas" or something like that (not sure how to spell it). Anyway, I don't think either of them will get a hiding now. If I don't get to go to McDonald's with Dad, I might have to give them both a thick ear!

Mum said she had a present for me, but because of the darts tragedy everyone else forgot about my birthday—except for Dad. He gave me this diary and said it was for me to write down my hopes and dreams. He also said it's the first step towards my university education. I'm not sure how that works. I'm only 13 now so it'll be a long time before I need to think about that. Anyway, I don't want to go university, I want to be an air hostess and work for NAC. I want to fly to Egypt and see the pyramids and the tombs. I s'pose NAC flies to Egypt. I wonder if I'll go on a DC-3, or a 737, or a Viscount?

What I really wanted for my birthday was these groovy white go-go boots that come up to your knees. The laces crisscross all the way up. Even the metal clips that hold the laces are groovy. I feel brassed off about the boots cause I know we can't afford them. I think I'll try to get an after-school job so I can buy them myself. I don't think I'll ever get them because they cost $12.99! Huh. That's my first hope and dream, to buy that pair of white go-go boots. I'll look just like Emma Peel off that show on TV—*The Avengers.*

Maybe Mum <u>is</u> still going to surprise me with the boots. I'll sleep with my fingers crossed all night.

By the way...did you know that...I am now OFFICIALLY a teenager!!!!

MONDAY, 21 June

We heard Tavita was a superstar at school today coz
everyone wanted to know what happened to him. I saw
his teacher when I was walking past the boys' school on
my way home and she asked me about it too. When I
told her, she just shook her head. I said, "Ah well, you
know how it is, one kid—one brain, two kids—half a
brain, three kids—no brain at all." She laughed heaps
and patted my shoulder and I laughed too. I felt a bit bad
stealing Dad's joke, but it was funny and I liked making
her laugh.

We all helped out when we got home because we
could see that Mum was still a bit upset about what had
happened to Tavita. I heard her talking to Archie's
mum over the fence. They said things like "Those kids
don't know how lucky they are" and "Things could have
ended very badly." Oh shoot, I didn't realise it was that
serious. Maybe I won't bother giving the boys a hard
time after all.

Yuck I **HATE!!!** boiled cabbage. Tea was great **except**
for the cabbage. My mum makes the best meatballs in

the world. She puts crushed pineapple, tomato sauce, and mixed herbs in them. YUMMMMM. Everyone was home and Dad said if we got stuck in and did the dishes and our jobs we could have a game of cards after tea. He also said we're still going to McDonald's, but we have to wait for the weekend.

Lenny and Lily said they would do the dishes, and Ethan and Tavita said they would fill the wood bucket and feed the pets. They said I could have a break because my birthday got mucked up yesterday. I got to watch the news with Mum and Dad (b-o-r-r-r-ring). I hate the news, I wish *Top Town* was still on, I loved that. I heard there's going to be a second series. I wonder how old you have to be to get into the teams? Whangarei won it this year, but I reckon if Porirua put a team in we would win. We could all eats heaps of McDonald's burgers and we'd be unbeatable!

When all the jobs were done, I got some fab presents. I'd been telling Mum about this thing our teacher brought to school. It was sort of like binoculars with round disks that slot into the top of it, and when you look through the two eyepieces, you see the pictures in 3D. I couldn't believe it. It was so amazing, it felt like you were in the picture. If you held the binoculars up to the light it was like the sun was shining and it didn't matter if you moved your head up or down, the pictures still looked the same. I loved it so much I asked Mr. Morrison if I could look at lunchtime. He could see I really liked it so he let me bring the binoculars home for the night. He has all these disks showing places all over the world. He even has disks about Egypt. I was so excited about that—until I looked at them and saw some mummified people. That was freaky! I don't think I want to go to Egypt now. I do want to go to Argentina though, it looks beautiful.

Mum saw how much I enjoyed it, so she got me one. It's called a View-Master and it came with a set of seven

cartoon disks in a little thing shaped like a film reel. Mum also got me another set of disks about Japan with 3 disks in that pack. Lenny must have gone with her because he bought me some too. It's a Disneyland set about Fantasyland. He said there's one for each land and that I can collect them all—Frontierland, Tomorrowland, Main Street U.S.A., Adventureland, and New Orleans Square. I wish I had the whole set. I hope I go to Disneyland one day. I bet that would cost heaps though. I think that's a dream. Anyway, Lily brought me some bath cubes and Ethan and Tavita got me 2 Big Charlies.

Goodnight, dear Diary. Sleep tight. Don't let the beds bugs bite!

P.S. Best thing is I won Last Card. What a super cool night.

P.P.S. The other best thing (cherry on top) is my View-Master.

TUESDAY, 22 June

Mr. Morrison said we have to do a speech about ourselves. We have to do it in front of the whole class and it has to be at least 2 minutes long. I think I'll be sick that day. I don't want to stand up in front of everyone and talk. Anyway, who wants to hear about my life? I'd rather eat cabbage than do that.

I like school. I love maths and art and story writing. Today in maths we played Buzz and I WON. I heard Charlotte Craig say, "Sofia always wins." I don't think she meant it in a good way because she had a mean look on her face. Colin Baker said, "You're just jealous, Charlotte harlot."

Charlotte went bright red and glared at me. It's not my fault Colin said that! I think Mr. Morrison heard but he never said anything. He probably knows that Charlotte's a bit mean sometimes. We have one week to prepare our speeches. What the heck am I supposed to say about myself?! Hmmm. I'll ask Mum and Dad.

WEDNESDAY, 23 June

I guess Colin thought he was helping when he said that stuff to Charlotte but all it's done is make her meaner. When I was walking down the corridor she was standing there with her friends as I walked past.

"Can anyone smell that?" she said, really loudly. "I think it's a Samoan stink."

Her stupid idiot friends laughed. I went bright red and wanted to punch her. I carried on walking, trying to act like I didn't care, but I did. Then in class she put her hand up and asked Mr. Morrison if he could smell an awful stink. Her idiot friends laughed again. I went red again. I wish she would leave me alone. I don't want to do my speech in front of them!

SATURDAY, 26 June

I finally got to go to McDonald's for lunch with Dad. Man, everything was so shiny and clean! It was bright yellow and red and there were tiles and chrome everywhere. It's the coolest thing I've ever seen. I thought it would be neat to get a job there so I asked the lady behind the counter and she said you have to be 16, darn it.

I had a Big Mac, fries, and a fizz. Dad had the same. Yummy-scrummy, no cabbage in these burgers! After lunch, Dad asked what else I wanted to do and I said the

Botanic Garden. I didn't think he'd say yes because it's a long way into Wellington and we usually all go together, but he did! We got an ice cream after the garden and went home. It was the BEST DAY.

SUNDAY, 27 June

I started my speech today.

"My Family and Me"

"My dad is Siaosi Savea. People call him Sid because they think Siaosi is too hard to say, which is kinda funny because the English equivalent is actually George, not Sid. He was born in Samoa and his parents still live there. Grandma and Grandpa's real names are Lilyana and Tavita. Dad works for Todd Motors, making cars. We tease him about one day bringing a new car home for us.

My mum is Mary-Rose Savea. She's a night cleaner. Her last name was Sparks before she married Dad. She is Pākehā and was born in Napier and her parents still live there. We call them Christama and Stanpa. It started because their names are Christina and Stan but when Ethan was little he couldn't say Grandma Christina and

Grandpa Stan. Instead he'd say Christama and Stanpa. It just stuck and we all like it.

Lenny is the oldest kid. He's 17 and named after my uncle Leonard (Mum's brother). He has a milk run. Lenny, that is, not Uncle Leonard.

My older sister Lily is 15. She's named after Grandma and her middle name is Pearl. Dad says it because pearls are precious.

Ethan is 10 and goes to Cannons Creek School. His best friend is Archie, our next-door neighbour. Sometimes they get into trouble together.

Tavita is 9 and goes to Cannons Creek School too. He's named after Dad's dad. He likes following Dad around and helping him make stuff. Tavita, that is, not Grandpa.

I am Sofia Christina Savea. I was given my middle name after Grandma Christina (Christama). Dad chose my first name. Mum says he chose it because of Sophia Loren (the actress). We have 2 cats, Jaffa and Minty, and a dog, Maile (Samoan for "dog"). I like art, maths, and writing."

I read it to Mum and Dad. They said the family bit was good but I needed to make stuff about me more interesting and make the speech longer, as it only took 1 minute and 10 seconds. They said I need to read it a bit slower too. Blow that! I plan to read it as quick as I can and get it over with. I'll try to add some more about me tomorrow.

MONDAY, 28 June

Mr. Morrison read us some short profiles about famous people today so we would have some ideas about what we might want to say about ourselves. That's all very well for those people—they're famous for the things they did, so there's plenty to say about them. What have we got to say? We're only 12 or 13!

I really liked the profile about Martin Luther King Jr., though. He was an African American who fought for civil rights for him and his people. He wanted the

Black people in America to be treated fairly and have the same rights as the white people. It's a really sad story because he was shot and killed for standing up for what he believed. The saddest part is that he had a wife and children. One of his children, Bernice, was

born the same year as me. Maybe when I'm an air hostess, I'll fly to America and meet her. That would be cool bananas and she could tell me about her father.

The other profile I liked was about Kate Sheppard. She got women the vote, making New Zealand the first country in the world to do it. I don't know why women couldn't vote before that. That's just unfair. Kate Sheppard was like Martin Luther King Jr., in a way, because she fought for people's rights too.

Walt Disney was also an interesting profile. Mr. Morrison said profiles should tell the audience about the person, what they believe, and what they did. Geez, I haven't done anything—and I believe what my parents tell me. This is going to be hard!

I'll have tea and then try to finish my speech.

CABBAGE again! WHY?

When we were doing the dishes, Tavita wanted to know what year he was born (1967). His teacher said they have to find out what was happening in the world the year they were born. It got me thinking about things that have happened in my life, and that helped with my speech. Here's what I've added:

"I was born 20th June 1963.

In 1964 I was a baby. I beleived in sleeping, drinking milk, and (when I was teething) eating rusks.

In 1965 I was 2. I beleived in following Dad around, saying "me too." (Mum said that was what I did, so sometimes they called me "me too."")

In 1967 I was 4. I beleived in being a big sister and playing with my baby brothers.

In 1968 I was 5. I beleived in going to school. (I didn't really beleive in this, I had to go. I was really scared about going but at least I had Lily with me.)

In 1972 I was 9. I beleived in Santa Claus (or I pretended to, so I didn't miss out).

In 1974 I was 11. I beleived in going to Intermediate. (Well, I had to go and it was scary because Lily wasn't there.)

In 1975 I was 12. I beleived in sunbathing and going to the swimming pool.

DAWN RAID

It's 1976 now. I have just turned 13. I beleive in going to College (yay, both Lily and Lenny are here), and I think I beleive in civil rights. The thing I beleive the MOST is that kids shouldn't have to eat cabbage—it should be banned!"

Mum and Dad said that was a clever way to talk about my life. They said it was still less than 2 minutes because I read it too fast. Dad reckons I could be a writer. I do love

reading books, especially scary ones. Tomorrow we have to do our speeches. My tummy is churning and I think I feel a bit sick about it. Maybe it's the flu? I wonder if I can fool Mum.

TUESDAY, 29 June

Nope. Mum didn't buy it. She said I don't have a temperature and I'd eaten breakfast just fine. I should've known better than to eat breakfast—whoops!

Mr. Morrison said we would do our speeches in alphabetical order, which was good and bad. Good because I wasn't first, bad because I had ages to wait and it made me nervous. I didn't even hear the 6 kids who went before me. Colin had to go first. I felt sorry for him, but he didn't even care. I think he likes talking in front of the class.

Charlotte must have been nervous because she read hers REALLY fast. Hers was a bit sad. She lives with her aunt and shares a room with 2 of her cousins. Her brother lives with another aunt, and her sister is with her mum. I don't get it, why wouldn't they all live with her mum?

When I read mine, I decided not to rush like Charlotte. Everyone laughed when I read the bit about the cabbage, even Charlotte and her stupid friends. We had to hand in our written speeches.

WEDNESDAY, 30 June

We got our speeches back and this is what Mr. Morrison wrote on mine:

"Good job, Sofia, this is well written and a creative way to talk about yourself. You have used humour and painted an interesting picture with your words. Your speech was well paced and you paused to get the attention of the audience. Be sure to check your spelling (remember, "i before e except after c") and the use of commas. You may be a writer in the making."

I was floating on a cloud when I read that. I fell off the cloud and hit the ground when I read his last comment though . . . "Would you like to read this out at assembly?"

NOOOOOOO, I would not like to read it in front of the whole school! NO WAY ~~HOSE HOSAY~~ JOSE (actually, I think this is how it's spelled, like the song "Do You Know the Way to San Jose").

Mum and Dad said they were chuffed with what Mr. Morrison wrote. Dad said I should read it out at assembly, he said I needed to push myself. The only place I want to push myself is off a cliff! I can't speak in front of the whole school! I actually do feel sick now.

THURSDAY, 1 July

I have to read my speech in assembly tomorrow. I practised tonight in front of everyone. I left out the bit about pretending to believe in Santa, of course, coz I didn't want to ruin it for the boys.

"I don't get in trouble with Archie," Ethan said. Mum gave him a look and pointed to Tavita's eye and that shut him up. Lenny said he liked the bit about Martin Luther

King Jr. and civil rights. He asked if I knew anything about the Māori land march.

"It started last year in the far north," he said, "from a place called Kapowairua. They headed south and collected more people from a marae Te Hapua."

The Māori people were unhappy because land had been taken from them by the government (the Crown, as Lenny called it) and never returned. Lenny told us their slogan is "Not one more acre of Māori Land."

"That sounds like a civil rights problem," I said. (I felt quite grown up saying that.) Lenny agreed and laughed. Dad didn't though. He got a bit annoyed with Lenny.

"It's nothing like what Martin Luther King died for. Those Māori are just stirring up trouble. They should leave it alone—it happened a long time ago."

Lenny wasn't going to leave it alone though. "Martin Luther King died fighting for justice for Black people—a battle they'd been fighting for hundreds of years. The Māori are only asking for things that were taken from them since the Pākehā came and the government started taking land illegally—"

Dad interrupted him. "Well, we need to move on. They need to make the most of what they have now and get on with it."

"So if someone took our family tapa cloth, you wouldn't try to get it back?" Lenny snapped.

Dad looked mad. "Don't be silly, of course I would."

"And if the people who took it wouldn't give it back, wouldn't it still be yours?"

Dad was quiet for a moment. I thought Lenny was crazy talking to him like this. Then Dad said, "It's a family treasure. We would do everything we could to get it back."

Lenny smiled. "Yes, Dad, that's exactly what the Māori say about their land."

Dad opened his mouth but no words came out.

There was a bit of an awkward moment, and then Mum said, "How about we make some doughnuts for supper?"

I felt sorry for Dad. I've never seen him lost for words. In the kitchen, Lenny told me more about the Māori land march. His friend Rawiri's family are Māori and are quite involved with the people who organised the march. It's called a hīkoi (pronounced "hee-coy"). I wonder if Dad's right. Also, what if the Māori try to take our house and land back? Wow—I didn't know writing about myself would start all this!

FRIDAY, 2 July

I can't eat my breakfast. Too scared about reading my speech in front of the whole school. Dad's gone to work and Mum won't be home from her shift for a while. I'm thinking of hiding under the house before she gets home. It's a long time to hide there all day, though . . . and it's really dusty and there's spiders. Oh man, I don't know what to do! The best thing about today is it's Friday so if I muck up my speech there's a whole weekend for everyone to forget about it. Better go to school.

Well, I'm still alive! I thought I was going to die at assembly. There were 3 of us reading our speeches. Me, Alice Reid from Room 7, and, to my BIG surprise, Lenny! When we were waiting to go on to the stage, I asked Lenny why he didn't tell us he was doing it too. He said Mr. Carter only told him this morning because he didn't want Lenny to get worked up about it. I think Mr. Carter should have a talk with Mr. Morrison. I spent 2 days being worked up about this! I asked Lenny if he was worried.

"Nah, I don't care. Anyway, it's a good speech, so why should I worry?"

Lenny's right, I thought. I shouldn't care either because Mr. Morrison, Mum, Dad, Lenny, Lily, and the boys all thought my speech was good too.

Alice went first—she was really good. Her story was about the most important events of the past ten years. She talked about the moon landing with Neil Armstrong, Michael Collins, and Buzz Aldrin. Buzz?? That's not even a real name, is it?

Then it was my turn. My mouth went dry when I saw the crowd. I've never stood on the stage and looked at the whole school, there are TONS of kids at my school. I was looking for Lily, but there were so many faces I stopped trying. I tried to pace myself and look at the audience. When I read the last bit, about the cabbage, everyone laughed and then the kids all clapped. I looked at Lenny and he was smiling at me and clapping too.

Lenny was my hero today. His speech was about the hīkoi (Māori land march). It was really interesting hearing why the Māori people are angry. When he asked questions like, "How would you feel if someone took something of yours without asking?" I saw some of the teachers nodding at each other. After assembly, I was stoked when Mr. Carter told me my speech was really good. THEN he said, "I'm organising a local schools' speech competition and I'd like you to enter for your age group."

Geez, that freaked me out! Then I thought how proud Lenny was of me and how I liked it when everyone laughed. I couldn't believe it when I opened my mouth and said, "Yes." OH MY GOSH, when will this all stop!

When I got home I watched TV—it was a big celebration coz it's been 1 year since TV2 started. It's so good having 2 channels I don't know how we managed with just one! I watched *Bewitched*. Tabitha's my favourite. She gets up to mischief all the time and her mum, Samantha, has to fix it. I wish I could do magic. I'd make an endless supply of vanilla milkshakes and nut roll bars. And I'd have a pair of go-go boots in every colour.

After tea, Dad made some doughnuts and we all watched the Donny and Marie Osmond show. Marie was wearing bright blue go-go boots—WOW, they looked so amazing—I want them!

We are really lucky to have a colour TV. We wouldn't have got it if Mum hadn't gone back to work because it cost $840—2 months' wages! They had to save hard to get it. But man, Marie's go-go boots look great in colour. Other kids love coming to our house to watch TV coz most of them still have black and white sets.

SATURDAY, 3 July

Mum let me sleep in today. It was almost 11 o'clock when I got woken up by the sound of clinking bottles and people talking outside my window. Sounded like people having a bottle drive. I got up to see what was happening, and when I opened the curtains there was Colin Baker staring back at me. I got such a fright I ducked down, which was stupid coz he'd already seen me, but I was so embarrassed, dressed in my pj's with sleep in my eyes and hair everywhere, looking gross.

What if he tells everyone at school? Oh man, I might have to change schools now! They were there for ages getting the bottles from under the house, so I crawled to the bathroom to wash my face. When I heard them move off, I went out for breakfast, still in my shorty pj's, and ran straight into Lenny and his friend Rawiri, who were sitting at the kitchen table. I got such a surprise I quickly tried to backtrack, but slipped on the freshly polished lino and landed on my bum. Rawiri rushed over to help me, but I was up and out of there before he could get close.

What a terrible start to the day. Bad enough that Colin saw me with messed-up hair, now Rawiri saw me fall flat on my BUM in my PYJAMAS. I got back into bed and pulled the bedspread over my head.

When Mum called me for lunch, I had to go out and face Rawiri. He just smiled. At least this time I was DRESSED.

Ethan and Tavita were sitting outside on the steps and I could see they'd been crying. Tavita's face looked shiny and sticky. I asked what happened but they both started bawling. I looked at Mum and she pointed to the kitchen rubbish bin that was now sitting on the front lawn. The whole lid and the side of it were melted. I could see Mum was upset—she only bought it a few weeks ago. It's really flash. You step on the pedal and the lid opens . . . well, it did!

Mum told me the boys AND ARCHIE were told to empty the rubbish into the big bin in the shed. They were mucking around out there when they found a petrol can. One of them had the great idea to use the petrol can to make a campfire! Oh yeah. The boys sent Tavita in to get some matches. Then they lit a match and dropped it into the petrol can, which was almost empty,

but the fumes exploded and Tavita got burnt. That's why his face was shiny and sticky—Mum had put cream on it, which Tavita calls "oinkment." Maybe he thinks it comes from pigs, haha.

Anyway, the firebomb (which is what Tavita and Ethan are calling it) set the net curtain in the shed on fire. The boys panicked and ripped it down and threw it in the rubbish bin, which is how the bin got melted. Dad heard all the noise and went running in, grabbed the bin, threw it on the lawn, and got the hose onto it. The bin is still sitting on the lawn and Ethan and Tavita are sitting on the step having to look at it. Archie got sent home—again. Kind of weird how trouble follows those boys around!

Dad made a chow mein for lunch with chicken and celery and pineapple in it. I was starving. It was sooooo scrummy. Ethan and Tavita were very quiet at lunch. They didn't eat all of theirs, so I finished both of them. Rawiri stayed for lunch and

told everyone how good Lenny was at public speaking. Then he looked over at me and said, "You're really good too, Sofia." I felt my face go a bit red.

Rawiri talked about Lenny's speech. Mum and Dad were really interested and even asked a few questions about the hīkoi. But when Rawiri said that all of us needed to stand up and let the government know that injustice is not okay, Dad said we all just need to get on with our lives and leave the government to do their job. Rawiri could see Dad was getting a bit tense, so he stopped talking about it.

After lunch, Ethan asked Mum what she wanted done with the chicken bones. She told him to put them in the bin. There was a pause . . . then we all laughed, except for Ethan. He started to cry. I think he felt bad that they'd ruined Mum's new bin—and that Tavita got hurt. Mum gave him a hug and told him to go have a lie down.

SUNDAY, 4 July

It was a hot day today. We don't get many hot days in the middle of winter, so me and Lily were sunbathing out the back. Rawiri came over again and he and Lenny came out and lay on the lawn too. It's weird—I was worried when Rawiri saw me in my shorty pj's but I didn't care when I was in my togs. Anyway, no one's looking at me with Lily sunbathing in her bikini. I know Rawiri noticed her because he started singing, "It was an itsy bitsy teenie weenie yellow polka dot bikini that she wore for the first time today . . ."

Lily just turned her transistor radio up and closed her eyes. She's so cool nothing ever really bothers her.

The boys were talking about Lenny's speech again and Rawiri said, "I think it's great that you are so interested in what's happened to the Māori people, but you also need to think about what's happening to the Islanders." (He meant Pacific Islanders, like Dad.) They were talking about a thing the government had been doing, called dawn raids. Me and Lily didn't know what they were talking about, so Rawiri explained.

"A couple of years ago, the government

decided there were too many Islanders who were here illegally so they started looking for them—by breaking into people's houses in the early hours of the morning . . . at dawn when everyone is in bed asleep. Sometimes they catch someone and deport them back to the Islands. The government was happy to have them when they wanted cheap labour, but now there's an economic crisis"(whatever that is!) "they've started these dawn raids again. Islanders are getting the blame for being a drain on society."

WOAH, this is heavy stuff, I thought. "How come you know so much about this and we know so little?" I said to Rawiri.

Lily even turned her transistor down at this point and sat up to listen. We asked Rawiri loads of questions about the dawn raids. Lily isn't usually interested in this sort of thing, so it was good we were all talking about it together.

"Do you think we might get dawn-raided because Dad's an Islander?" I asked.

Lenny said, "Us kids are Islanders too."

"But we aren't real Islanders like Dad," I said.

We all argued for a bit about whether we are real Islanders or not. Rawiri broke it up saying, "The dawn raids are mainly happening in Auckland, and they're targeting people who are overstayers." Realising I didn't know what he meant, he said, "That means they've come into the country without having the right paperwork, or they DID have the paperwork but have overstayed their permits."

"So how does the government know who is an overstayer and who isn't?" Lily asked.

"Sometimes they don't."

"So why did the government let so many Islanders in if it was going to cause a problem?" said Lily.

"After the war, in the 1940s I think, there was a shortage of workers, so the government relaxed the immigration laws to let more people from the Islands come in to do the factory and labouring jobs."

Huh, that's funny, Dad works in a factory. I don't think it's fair that the government is calling Islanders a "drain on society." My dad works really hard and he's an Islander, and all his mates work really hard too. Oh my gosh, I wonder if Dad has a permit thingy? Maybe someone should talk to him about this. Rawiri also said the government and the media are making it look like Polynesians are taking all the jobs and being violent lawbreakers. He said it's stereotyping (not sure exactly what that means but I guess we'll learn more about it in our typing class at school). THAT IS SO UNFAIR, my dad's not violent and he would NEVER break the law.

Archie's mum brought him over and made him give all his pocket money to Mum to put towards a new bin. Archie was crying, but I'm not sure if it was because he was sorry about the bin or sorry about losing his pocket money.

Lenny had to get ready for his milk run so Rawiri dropped him off.

I got sunburnt.

MONDAY, 5 July

Everyone at school was nice to me about my speech. Mr. Morrison congratulated me in front of the class for being selected for the speech competition. Blow it—I forgot about that, I haven't even told Mum and Dad about it yet. Mr. Morrison said I had to see Mr. Carter at lunchtime about the competition details. That made me feel a bit sick again. I wonder how many people will be at the competition.

Mr. Morrison told the class that since we've been learning about each other with our speeches we'll be having a cultural food day, and we need to bring some food from our culture to share with the class. We had to talk to each other about what foods are important to our families, then we went around the class sharing 3 special foods each. It's funny, I used to be scared to speak up in class, but since I did my speech onstage I'm not even worried about sharing my ideas with everyone anymore.

Colin was first again, not because of alphabetical order, but because he put his hand up first. He loves speaking up in class. He said his important family foods were roast dinners, meatballs, and cheese rolls. No one knew what cheese rolls were so he told us his mum is from a place called Gore, way down south, where they make cheese rolls by rolling grated cheese up in a piece of bread. They toast them in the oven and spread heaps of butter on them. They sound weird but yummy. I think I prefer scones.

Then Colin said, "Our Scout group did a bottle drive in the weekend . . ."

I felt a moment of panic and started hearing a ringing sound in my ears.

"It was fun," he went on. "We raised a heap of money and we got to see some really nice people." He was looking straight at me. I went BRIGHT RED!

Mr. Morrison laughed at Colin and said, "That's good to hear, Colin, but let's keep on track." Thank goodness for Mr. Morrison.

When it was my turn, I told the class the important foods in my family are my dad's Samoan chop suey, pineapple pie, and cornbeef stew. When everyone finished, Mr. Morrison said we had to say which food we thought we might bring. I said cornbeef stew. I chose this because it takes less time to make than the other things and I think Mum or Dad would help me with it.

As I walked past Charlotte and her lot at morning teatime, she said, quite loudly, "Cornbeef stew, who would bring that cat food to a class lunch?" I heard her idiot friends laugh and then it was a bit of a blur . . . I felt my stomach burn . . . and the next thing I knew, I'd pushed Charlotte into the lockers. There was a lot of yelling from her friends, and loads of other kids came running over.

Charlotte must have got a real fright from my shove, because before I knew it, she'd shoved me and I tripped backwards and fell over. As I was getting up she swung her fist and hit me on the cheek. Next thing, we were in a full-blown fight. Other kids were yelling, "Scrap! Scrap!"

Two duty teachers broke us up and sent the other kids packing. I started to cry then, and so did Charlotte. We got sent to the office and had to wait for the principal.

We didn't even get to tell him our sides of the story. We just got a huge telling-off and warned that our parents would be very disappointed in us.

I couldn't believe it when Charlotte mumbled, "Mine won't."

Mr. Arbuckle got a bit angry with her. "I assure you, young lady, they will."

THEN Charlotte said, "I assure you, Mr. Arbuckle, they won't. My father is dead and my mother is up north."

38

Well, that stopped Mr. Arbuckle in his tracks. I'd forgotten that Charlotte lived with her aunt. He raised his voice then, and it got a bit squeaky. "Back to class, both of you, and no more fighting."

It was embarrassing walking back into the classroom. We both went to our desks, got our maths books out, and pretended to be working. Well, I pretended, and I guess Charlotte did too.

I decided not to tell Mum and Dad what happened, but when I got home and looked in the mirror I had a huge bruise on my cheek and scratch marks on my face and neck. What a catty fighter that Charlotte is!

Everyone wanted to know what happened to me. I thought I was fine about it until I opened my mouth to tell them, and I burst out crying! When I finally got it out, Dad just shook his head. Mum was a bit wide-eyed and I could see she was shocked. Mr. Arbuckle was right, though—they were disappointed.

"Sometimes you just need to ignore things people say," Dad said.

I sure wish I had.

Maybe tomorrow will be a better day.

OH NO, I forgot to see Mr. Carter about the speech competition. Oh well, it's probably for the best. I don't feel like speaking in front of anyone with my face all bashed up and scratched.

TUESDAY, 6 July

Tavita's face has blistered, so Mum took him to the doctor today. Mum said the doctor told him off, and of course he bawled (Tavita, not the doctor). What a bunch of sooky-la-las we all are—one of us always seems to be crying.

Mr. Carter pulled me out of class to talk about the speech competition. He said I was lucky still to be involved, because of the fight. I wanted to tell him he was lucky I was going to do it, but I didn't. He said I can talk about anything I want but it has to be a 5-minute speech. Holey moley!!!! That's a long time to talk!

I was about to tell him I didn't want to do it, then he told me there are cash prizes—and all I could think of was my go-go boots. The competition is ages away, in November, so I have tons of time.

WEDNESDAY, 7 July

School was cool bananas today. We had a guy come and teach us some Māori stuff. His name is Mr. Parker, and he was really fun. I think he's related to Charlotte—he kept calling her "girl" and getting her to show us stuff. Charlotte was really good at it too. He taught us some songs and then we did a stick game. The sticks are called "rakau," which means stick or tree. I liked the songs. The first one was called "Tutira Mai Nga Iwi," which we all sort of knew. Here are the words:

Tūtira mai ngā iwi (all the boys say "AUE" here, it sounds like this: "oh-way")

tātou tātou e

Tūtira mai ngā iwi (they do "AUE" here too)

tātou tātou e

DAWN RAID

Whai-a te marama-tanga

me te aroha—e ngā iwi!

Ki-a tapa tahi,

Ki-a ko-tahi rā

Tātou tātou e

(we sing it all again)

Tā-tou tā-tou e!! (the girls hold on to the last "eee"
sound here)

Tahi, rua, toru, whā

kssss . . . hi aue hei (the boys or a leader does
this bit)

This is what it means:

Line up together, people

All of us, all of us

Stand in rows, people

All of us, all of us

Seek after knowledge

and love of others—everyone

Think as one

Act as one

All of us, all of us

All of us, all of us!

One, two, three four

The "kssss hi aue hei" part is just how we finish. It sounds really good when we all finish this part loud and in time. We flick our fingers in the air at ksss he aue and then end with our hands on our hips at hei. Mr. Parker said it's a good song because it's about standing together and uniting as one, shoulder to shoulder. He told us it was written by a friend of his called Wi Huata, who wrote it to teach his children about supporting each other. Apparently they were at a family gathering at Lake Tutira, up Napier way.

I didn't even know there was a lake called Tutira. Maybe Christama and Stanpa will take us there when we visit them. If I ever go there, I'm going to sing the song to the lake.

Mr. Parker said songs or waiata belong to the people and groups who compose them, and we need to respect the people who wrote them by singing them well. He told the boys that the bit where they go "AUE" was okay, but he thought they could do better. When we sang it the second time the boys did their part really strongly and Mr. Forbes the caretaker came to see what all the noise was about.

The boys were pretty pleased with themselves and Mr. Parker gave them the thumbs-up and smiled. Then we learnt the rakau (stick) games. Mr. Parker had a whole set of rakau for us to use, that he'd made out of rolled-up magazines. We had to find a partner and then he went through all the actions, bit by bit. I was partners with Tania. I like working with her, she's nice.

First, we just kept tapping our rakau to a beat, then we did some tapping to each side, then tapping our rakau on our partner's rakau and then . . . things got crazy when we had to learn how to pass the rakau to each other. Rolled-up magazines were flying in all directions! What a laugh!

Once we knew all the actions and the order they went in, Mr. Parker taught us a song called "E Papa Waiari." When we had it all sorted, Mr. Parker sang the song and called out the actions. I couldn't believe it when Mr. Morrison said it was time to pack up. The afternoon just zoomed by.

When I got home, I made some rakau and taught Lily. Good fun! The boys wanted to join in so we made them some. Mum and Dad knew the song, too, so after tea we made more rakau and all did it together. Rawiri was there again, which was good because he knew the song too, and he could partner Tavita, and Lenny was with Ethan. The rolled-up magazines were okay, but some were fat and some were skinny so it made it a bit harder.

So Dad went out to the shed and found some old broom handles, which he cut into lengths for us to use. They were perfect and were all the same fatness. We did the "E Papa Waiari" song a few more times. Mum was really good at it.

Later, Mum made pikelets for supper. FUN night!

Then Back To Step 1!

THURSDAY, 8 July

I took some of my rakau to school and used them at morning tea and lunchtime. Me, Tania, Colin, and his friend Walter. Mr. Morrison thought my rakau were great and said I should decorate them. Then he suggested that all the class should make their own and we could paint them. Dad was stoked that Mr. Morrison liked his idea.

After tea I saw Rawiri pull up in his mum's car. I was thinking how cool it was that he can drive and that his mum lets him use the car. Next thing . . . I got the shock of my life when Charlotte Craig, the cattiest catfighter in the world, got out of the car!!! What??! Then I remembered that Charlotte lived with her auntie because her mum was up north. Rawiri had told us his aunt and cousin had something to do with the people who organised the hīkoi up north. That's when I realised—OH MY GOLLY GOSH—Rawiri and Charlotte are cousins!

I rushed to my room and pretended to be reading a book. I thought I was safe there—until Rawiri and Lenny appeared at the bedroom door . . . with Charlotte.

I guess she hadn't figured out me and Lenny were brother and sister either. Her face went bright red when she saw me and she took a step back. I tried to act cool and said, "Hi," and carried on reading. Lenny said they were going to the dairy and I could come if I wanted.

"Nah, I'm okay, thanks," I said. Then Lily poked her head around the corner and said she'd go. And I didn't want to miss out, so I suddenly said, "Oh, okay, I'll come too."

I ended up sitting beside Charlotte in the car and I could see she had a scratch down her neck. I didn't know I was a catty fighter too. It *was* my first fistfight—or should I say, "fingernail fight."

"Who's your teacher?" Lily asked Charlotte.

"Mr. Morrison."

Lily looked surprised, and said, "Oh, so you guys know each other then?"

We both said, "Uh-huh," and looked in opposite directions. I think that's when Lily realised what was going on and changed the subject. She asked Charlotte if she liked the Bay City Rollers, and then we all started talking about our favourite songs.

When we got to the dairy we got a milkshake each (I got vanilla, my fave), then played a game where you had to say your favourite song, and whoever guessed the singer or the band first got a point. We sat outside at a table and Lenny brought some milkshake lollies which we used for points.

We chose 3 songs each. Mine were "Boogie Fever" by the Sylvers, "Deep Purple" by Donny and Marie, and "Silly Love Songs" by Wings. Lily chose "Don't Go Breaking My Heart" by Elton John and Kiki Dee (I love that one too), "Kiss and Say Goodbye" by the Manhattans, and "Rhiannon" by Fleetwood Mac. Charlotte chose "Only 16" by Dr. Hook, "December, 1963" by the Four Seasons, and "A Little Bit More," Dr. Hook again.

I think the boys were just being jerks coz they chose songs like "You Sexy Thing" and "Let Your Love Flow." Lenny chose "Disco Duck" and we all started to sing it and make the duck sound. So funny. Talk about laugh! The dairy owner told us off for being too noisy and said we had to tone it down. Lily ended up with the most lollies so she won.

We were having so much fun that I forgot Charlotte was a chump. Rawiri said a real test of whether an artist is any good or not will be if they're still around producing music in 20 years. Woah! That would be a long time doing the same thing.

Then I remembered something. "Charlotte," I asked, "are you related to Mr. Parker?"

"Hmm, dunno really. I call him 'uncle' but I'm not sure if we're actually related."

Rawiri told us that Charlotte lives with them because her mum's up north (which I already knew from Charlotte's speech). Lily asked Charlotte when her mum would be back, but Charlotte said she didn't know. She saw her in October last year when she was here with the protesters for the hīkoi. Rawiri went on to explain that Charlotte's mum had an important job helping to organise things for protest marches, so it was just easier for Charlotte to stay with his family. I wasn't sure if Charlotte was very happy for me to hear all about her life.

I don't think I could be away from my mum for that long. I felt a bit sorry for Charlotte when I heard that. Maybe that's why she's mean sometimes. I remember hearing about the protesters on the news—tons of people from up north marched through Porirua on their way to Parliament.

"Is your mum an activist?" Lily asked.

"Kinda, I guess. Her job on the march was to help organise where the marchers would stay at places along the way. She reckons it was a huge job because when the hīkoi

49

started there were fifty people, but by the time it arrived in Wellington there were about five thousand!"

"WOAH!" I said. "That's a heap of people to feed."

"Yeah, it was pretty exciting being involved in such a huge march," said Lenny.

WHAT ON EARTH?! Man, I didn't know Lenny had joined the march! No wonder he'd been so interested in talking about the hīkoi with all of us.

My brother is a PROTESTER. This is big news.

When I looked at Lily to see what she thought, she didn't seem surprised at all. "You knew about this, didn't you?" I said. She just smiled.

Lenny told us how he came to join the march. Rawiri had told him when the hīkoi was leaving Porirua, and Lenny stayed at Rawiri's the night before so he could go. He said it was a far-out experience to be part of something so big and important. They walked right along the motorway! It took 7 hours. People tooted at them and cheered, but some people shouted out mean things. He said there was heaps of cool singing along the way. I remember watching this on the news and Dad shaking his head.

Lenny said he was blown away by the people who had walked the whole hīkoi. He said Dame Whina Cooper, the leader of the hīkoi, is around 80 years old.

Te Hāpua

1,000 kilometres!!
620 miles!!

Wellington

She didn't walk all of the Porirua to Wellington part which Lenny and Rawiri joined for, but she was driven alongside to encourage people. Lenny reckons she's such a good leader. He said that if the government hadn't received the petition they brought with them then Dame Whina was going to give her "Dame" thingy back. Geez, that's a bit rad.

When they got to Parliament it was 2:00 p.m. and there was a massive crowd of people to welcome them. There was even a Māori group performing and Lenny said the energy was electric as they approached.

I still can't believe my brother Lenny is a protester! I feel really proud of him. It's so cool that Rawiri and Lenny talk to us about this stuff.

On the way home we sang "Burning Bridges," "Billy Don't Be a Hero," and "The Night Chicago Died." I love those songs and I know all the words.

Oh, and guess what? Lenny said his boss is looking for more kids to do milk runs and asked Lily if she wanted one. I told him I'd do it, but Lenny said you have to be 14. Bummer. Lily said she didn't want to coz she has loads of babysitting. I wish I could do it, I want to earn my own money.

SATURDAY, 10 July

Lenny asked if I wanted to go to the flicks with him and Rawiri. Charlotte's going too. I felt a bit nervous about it because, although things have been better between me and Charlotte, I don't know if I want to go to the movies with her and be "best buds." But the movie was *Logan's Run* and I really wanted to see it so I said yes. It was such a good movie too—tense and exciting, and very futuristic.

We hung out at our house after the movie, and Rawiri told us one of his friends from the hīkoi was coming to Porirua. His name is Tigilau—they call him Tigi ("Tingy") and he's an Islander. Lenny said he'd met him too, after the hīkoi. Tigi and some mates stayed and camped on the steps and in the grounds of Parliament. Tigi and his wife have a little baby and he camped there with them! Man, I bet that was hard work with a baby.

"Do you think your dad would like to meet Tigi?" Rawiri wondered. We said probably not because we don't think Dad believes in the hīkoi and stuff like that. Lenny said that Tigi is a "Polynesian Panther," and that he and some of his mates are coming to talk to Rawiri about becoming a Panther too. Have to say I'm a bit worried about this. It sounds like Tigi's in a gang and I know Dad and Mum won't like Lenny hanging around with a gang. I hope Lenny doesn't get in trouble.

WEDNESDAY, 14 July

We got a new kid in our class today. He's from Samoa and his name is Jonathan. Mr. Morrison asked Colin to look after him. Luckily he speaks good English (Jonathan I mean, not Colin). He joined our rakau group so the boys had to figure out how to do rakau with 3 people. They made up their own routine. When Mr. Parker came to do more Māori stuff with us, Mr. Morrison told him about the rakau my dad made. Mr. Parker really liked them. "Ka pai," he told me. Then he showed us some patterns we could use to decorate them and told us what they mean.

I think I'll use the hei matau (fishhook), coz it means prosperity or good fortune—so maybe it'll get me a job. Mr. Parker watched our rakau routines and said we're doing great. Mr. Morrison said maybe we could show our routines in assembly. NO THANKS,

Mr. Morrison, I've had enough of doing things in front of people! But of course we have Colin in our group and he loves showing off so he was keen as anything.

"How about we give Jonathan a chance to settle in before we ask him to get onstage in front of the whole school?" said Mr. Morrison.

"It's okay, sir," Jonathan said. "I don't mind."

He's a good sport. Tania and I told the boys they can do it.

THURSDAY, 15 July

Mr. Morrison is reading us a chapter book. When he got to a bit where someone was beckoning to someone else, he asked who could put "beckoning" into a sentence. Jonathan (the new Samoan kid) put up his hand and Mr. Morrison picked him. Jonathan said, "In the beckoning, God created the Earth." We looked at each other to see if we thought Jonathan was serious and then everyone in the class burst out laughing. Mr. Morrison couldn't hold it in either—he put the book up to his face but we could see his whole body shaking as he tried to hold his laughing in.

Jonathan must have realised what was going on and he started to laugh as well (thank goodness). Mr. Morrison kept trying to apologise to Jonathan but every time he opened his mouth, all that came out was a sort of wheezing sound and he had tears rolling down his face too. Every time Mr. Morrison thought he was okay to carry on reading, he would crack up again. It was nearly lunchtime so he just shooed us outside.

Our group had lunch with Jonathan and told him what beckoning meant. He's such a good sport, he said he was happy he gave the class a good laugh. After lunch Mr. Morrison said sorry to Jonathan and hoped he hadn't hurt his feelings.

"It's okay, Mr. Morrison," Jonathan said, "if you ever need another laugh, just beckon me over." Haha. How cool is that. I can see Jonathan's going to be popular.

FRIDAY, 16 July

I almost died of embarrassment today! There was our usual crew—me, Tania, Colin, Walter, and Jonathan—practising our rakau routine. We were trying something new where we all worked as one team, passing the rakau to the person beside us. Anyway, Walter got a rakau in the head and we all started to laugh really hard and then . . . I blew off! Everyone laughed even harder and so did I, but that made me let off again! I went bright red and hid my face in hands.

Colin said, "Don't worry, Sofia, that's nothing—listen to this," and he leaned over and did a huge fart. That started a chain reaction and Walter farted too. We all fell about laughing until my stomach ached. I have brothers so I know boys can blow off on demand, but

I never thought they'd do it at school! School has been fun this week.

SUNDAY, 18 July

Today was AMAZING. Lenny took me and Lily with him to a meeting at Rawiri's house, and I got to meet Rawiri's friend Tigi and his baby, Che (pronounced "Shay"). There were some other people from Wellington there as well as Tigi's lot.

When Tigi and the others arrived, Charlotte shrieked, and that's when I realised that her mum and sister were with them. There were lots of hugs and kisses and some tears as well. Charlotte was so pleased to see her mum, she didn't seem to care about us seeing her cry. Her mum even gave me a kiss on the cheek and a hug. It was a tight hug and I could feel that she really meant it, it was nice.

While everyone was having a cup of tea, I got to hold baby Che and he fell asleep on my knee. Cute! Then Tigi started telling us about the dawn raids. Apparently, the raids started in 1974 and they were called "Operation Pot Black." It was exactly like what Rawiri had told us—the police were breaking into Pacific Islanders' houses in the middle of the night or the early hours of the morning, which is why they're called "dawn raids." Mr. Muldoon's government have stepped up the dawn raids again because the economy is in bad shape and Islanders are getting the blame. They're being harassed on the streets and in the pubs and billiard halls, just because their skin is brown.

Tigi reckons it doesn't matter if you're Samoan or Niuean (like him), Tongan or Māori, the police will ask you to produce your passport or identification papers.

"Bloody thugs," one of the older guys said.

Tigi said some police officers don't want to do it but the government is making them blitz the Islanders. Lenny wondered how the Māoris feel, being treated like this in their own country. Tigi said they're angry too. It's a fascist government, he says. (I have no idea what that means but it doesn't sound good.)

One of the guys there told us that he and his friend were at the pub playing darts and the police came in and asked for their papers. He said one of the cops had a South African accent so his friend said to the cop, "How about you show us your papers first? I'm Māori and I was born here." And he carried on, speaking in Māori.

The cop got angry and told him to speak properly. He said, "I am. It's not my fault you're too ignorant to understand the language of the country you're living in." They both got arrested.

Charlotte surprised me when she said, "Sofia—you know who he's talking about, don't you?" I had no idea. "Uncle Piripi—I mean, Mr. Parker."

Man, I was so shocked! Poor Mr. Parker, he's such a nice man. He shouldn't be treated like that. No one should. Tigi says we're all part of the revolution and we need to stand up and fight back. Ummmmm, I'm not sure Dad would agree with that!

Tigi has a huge Afro. I expected him to be a scary gang member but it turns out the Polynesian Panthers aren't like that. Tigi told us some of the things they do, like starting homework clubs to help kids, helping old people with their gardens, and teaching people about their rights, especially if they get bullied by the police. Sometimes they hold demonstrations to protest against stuff. He also told us about the Black Panthers in America and how the Polynesian Panthers have been inspired by them. Tigi said the Panthers focus on people's rights and helping them to have a fair and better life. He said the panther is an important symbol for their group because a panther only attacks if it's attacked first. Fair enough.

Here's a picture I cut out from one of the Polynesian Panthers' pamphlets.

After the meeting, me and Charlotte went outside. We found some fizzy drink bottles stacked up at the side of the house and Charlotte asked her aunt if we could go cash some in. Her aunt said we could have a few each so off we went to the store. We got 4 Goofy bubblegums for each bottle. On the way home we opened a few and read the jokes. They were a bit dumb but the bubblegum was good.

"What about those dawn raids?" I said to Charlotte. "How mean is that?"

She said it's good that people like Tigi are helping Islanders stand up for themselves. Lots of them have spent days in jail cells because they couldn't show their paperwork.

That reminds me, I still need to ask Dad if he has his paperwork sorted. Charlotte knows a lot about what's going on with Māori and Island people. Her whole family does. Maybe Dad <u>would</u> like to meet them?

Once we got back from the shop, we had to go home coz Lenny had to do his milk run. I told Lenny I really wanted a milk run and that I would work hard. He said he'd ask his boss but he was pretty sure he would say no, coz I'm too young.

We all watched the Sunday night Disney movie called *Now You See Him, Now You Don't*. It was funny, I really liked it—about a teenager who invents an invisibility serum. Man, I'd love to have some of that!

I love the song at the start of all the Disney movies, which goes: "When you wish upon a star, makes no difference who you are . . ."

Today was a good day. Lots of fun things happened.

WEDNESDAY, 21 July

Mr. Parker came to class again today. He taught us a new song and then we did the ones we already know. Everyone is into rakau now. Kids are making their own out of magazines and bringing them to school. Mr. Parker is very pleased that we all like rakau so much and he thinks we're the best class in school at using them. Me and Tania did the whole song without dropping the rakau once.

Just before he left, I heard Mr. Parker ask Charlotte when Tigi and the others were heading home. I forgot that they all know each other. She told him they're leaving on Saturday. I guess her mum will be going with them—poor Charlotte.

An amazing thing happened today though! Dad went to the pub with his mates after work (no, that's not the amazing thing). He was having a beer and a game of pool and they got talking to some guys his friend knew called Piripi and Tigi! Dad found out that Piripi (Mr. Parker) has been teaching us rakau at school, and Mr. Parker found out that Dad was the one who made the wooden rakau that he liked. They also realised that Tigi was staying with Rawiri and his family so that was all pretty cool.

How about that? Dad met Tigi and Mr. Parker on his own. I don't think he knows Tigi is a Polynesian Panther though.

THURSDAY, 22 July

Oh, no. Things are not good. Lenny, Lily, and me got in massive trouble with Mum and Dad for going to Rawiri's house for the meeting with Tigi. It turned out one of Dad's friends was at the meeting, and he told Dad it was good to see us there and asked if Dad would be coming to the next one. When Dad's friend told him what the meeting was about, Dad was **NOT** happy. He said he wanted to talk to the 3 of us when Lenny got home from his milk run.

It was awful. Dad said how disappointed he was in all of us for going to the meeting and not telling him and Mum about it. Oh my gosh, it was only a meeting! Dad and Mum would have a mental if they knew Lenny had been in the hīkoi.

We tried to tell Dad about why the meeting was important but he just said we're asking for trouble if we hang out with troublemakers. We tried to tell them how the Polynesian Panthers help Islanders in all sorts of ways, but Dad wouldn't listen. As far as he's concerned, they're just a gang who is causing trouble instead of getting on with their lives.

I didn't want to argue with Dad, but I thought he was being unfair, so I said, "Dad, do you know that panthers only attack when they are attacked first?"

Well, that didn't help. Dad got really angry and said, "These people are filling your head with a load of nonsense."

Lenny got angry then. "When will you get it, Dad? They're doing what is right for our people. They are the ones who are standing up to the government and telling them they can't treat people unfairly."

"I know all about the Black Panthers in America." Dad was nearly shouting at Lenny now. "They're a gang that makes all sorts of trouble for the police. You can't tell me the Polynesian Panthers are any different. They're all gangs, and if you hang around with them, you will end up in jail!"

Lenny started to yell at Dad himself, saying, "That's the point, Dad! Pacific Islanders ARE ending up in jail, for no reason other than the government making them targets and blaming them for the downturn in the economy."

I couldn't help myself. I had to jump in too. "But, Dad—you met Tigi and Mr. Parker at the pub the other night. They're trying to help the Islanders who are being picked on. You met them, you know they're good people."

Dad yelled back: "Lenny, you should never have taken your sisters there. And you girls should know better than to hang out with these people!"

Lenny stood up and said, "You aren't even listening to what we're saying."

"SIT DOWN!" Dad yelled. "I'm telling all three of you that you will NOT be going back to that house, or to any more meetings."

"I'm almost 18!" Lenny shouted. "I can decide for myself who and what I support."

Dad stood up too, and said in a quiet voice, through clenched teeth, "Don't . . . talk . . . to me . . . like that."

Lenny stopped for a moment and no one knew what was going to happen next. Then Lenny sat down. THANK GOODNESS!

Mum and Lily let out a little breath and I could see they were both relieved, like I was. After the fight, we all got sent to our rooms. Me and Lily were upset. We talked for a bit about why Dad won't listen to what we're saying. Lily reckons he just doesn't understand what's going on. I told her I wanted to ask Dad if he had the right paperwork to be here, but now I'm too scared in case it fires him up again. Lily said she was sure he does, otherwise he wouldn't be able to work and stuff like that. I felt a bit better then. Lily always knows what to say to make people feel better.

I don't think we'll be seeing Tigi and the crew again. It's a shame, I liked hanging out with them, and playing with baby Che.

Lenny poked his head in the door later and said he'd asked his boss if I could have a milk run, and told him I'm a good worker. His boss had asked if I was good at maths for giving change and stuff.

"You know I'm really good at maths," I said.

"Yep, I told him that. And guess what? He said that you can do a one-week trial to see if you can manage all the heavy lifting."

Oh shoot, I thought, now I'll have to ask Mum and Dad—and at the moment I don't think they will be saying yes to anything.

Lenny said I could start on Sunday if I was allowed. Looks like I have 2 days to get Mum and Dad to say yes. I really really really—to infinity and back—want this milk run. I need my own money.

FRIDAY, 23 July

Grrr. Why are my little brothers so stupid? Mum and Dad must feel pretty disappointed in their kids this week. They've been up to the hospital AGAIN with Tavita. Mum said the doctor made her feel like a bad mother when he said, "I see you were here a month ago with Tavita." Except he pronounced it, "Tar-vie-tah." Mum said yes, but he's had another accident. Apparently the doctor raised an eyebrow, and that's why Mum was annoyed with him.

Dad didn't see it and thought she was reading too much into it, but Mum was pretty sure the doctor was implying that she doesn't look after her kids properly. Dad said, "You can't watch kids every minute of every day."

This time, the boys had been playing in the shed. Ethan had learnt to do a hangman's noose—I don't know who taught him or why—and he had made one for Tavita to try. (I know!) He helped Tavita onto a stool, tied his hands together, then put the noose around his neck. They were playing Sinbad the Sailor, apparently. Ethan said, "Take that, you swine," and kicked the stool away, which left Tavita hanging there by his neck, kicking. Ethan realised straightaway that this was a bad idea (no kidding!) and rushed to help Tavita, but didn't know what to do, so he started screaming for Mum.

Mum and Dad came running. When they got there, Ethan was holding Tavita up by his legs. Mum got such a fright she got all woozy and fainted, hitting her face on the shed doorway on her way down. Dad rushed over and lifted Tavita up. He was able to hold him up with one arm and loosen the knot with his other hand. Tavita's face was bright red and he had

rope burns on his
neck. Dad could see
Tavita was breathing
so he put him down
and rushed over to Mum,
who was starting to unfaint. He
yelled at Ethan to get Mum a drink of water, but
Ethan was so shocked, he just stood there. Dad yelled
at him again, then Ethan spewed—all over Mum's
feet!

Once everyone had got themselves together, Dad
checked that they were all okay. Tavita said his neck hurt
real bad at the back so Mum and Dad decided to take
him to the hospital, in case something was broken. I
thought if you got a broken neck you just died.

Poor Mum, she had to sit in the waiting room with a
cut cheek, spew on her shoes, and a kid with rope burns
on his throat. No wonder that doctor gave her the

stink-eye. I'm so glad I didn't have to go to the hospital with them.

Me and Lily stayed home to look after Ethan. He was so scared about what was going to happen to him this time. Lily was great. She told him it would be okay, that he would probably get a telling-off, but maybe it would help him to think about things in the future and be more sensible. I didn't say it, but I was just thinking, You are such an idiot, Ethan.

When they got home from the hospital, Mum looked exhausted. Dad called Ethan over and we all thought, Uh-oh, but then Dad just gave him a hug. In some ways, I think this was worse than a hiding or a telling-off, coz Ethan started blubbing and he couldn't stop. Me and Lily made Mum and Dad a cup of tea and some plates of banana on toast for everyone.

Then Dad asked where Lenny was. I hadn't even thought about Lenny, with everything that was going on, but now I realised he hadn't come home after his milk run. Lily must've known where he was coz she said he'd gone to the dairy to get some milk. Mum and Dad must have been too tired to even think properly and they just nodded. But why would Lenny need to go out for milk when he has a milk run and we get a free bottle every day? When he came in about 10 minutes later, Mum and Dad didn't seem to notice he wasn't carrying any milk. It must've been a tough day for them, poor Mum and Dad.

Oh, and it's Mum and Dad's wedding anniversary today—they've been married for 19 years. It's not very fair they had to spend their anniversary at the hospital and have toast for dinner.

SATURDAY, 24 July

Finally! Things are getting better. Three fantastic things happened today:

1. We got a letter from Samoa. Grandma and Grandpa are coming to New Zealand. They're going to be in Auckland with Uncle Joe, Dad's brother. (Joe's not his real name. Actually, I'm not even sure what it is!)

2. Dad said we are going on a family holiday to Auckland to see Grandma and Grandpa. YAY! They'll be there in October, so the best part is, it's not school

holidays so we're going to get extra time off school. We might be in Auckland for a couple of weeks, Dad says. It's so exciting! We leave on the 10th of October, so Lenny will have his 18th birthday up there. Cool.

3. Since Dad and Mum are all happy about the holiday, I figured it was a good time to ask if I could do a milk run with Lenny. They thought about it for a while, and when I told them I'd still work hard at school, and do my chores, they said I could do the trial.

I'm SO happy right now. I'm going to have my own money! I'll save hard so I can buy those boots for when we go on holiday to Auckland.

Lenny and Rawiri were sitting on the steps talking when I went to tell them about the milk run. Lenny said I have to be ready at 4:00 p.m., when the milk truck comes past to pick us up. I asked what I should wear and he said there's a lot of running and carrying heavy stuff, so I'd have to wear something suitable.

I could see that Rawiri and Lenny wanted to talk more so I left them alone. I bet they were talking about wherever it was that Lenny went yesterday. I reckon he was at another PP meeting. I hope Dad doesn't figure it out or there will be a gigantic fight.

I can't wait to start my milk run tomorrow! I'm going to work <u>so hard</u> to make sure I keep this job. I'll go to bed early tonight so I get tons of rest.

SUNDAY, 25 July

Man, I'm so foofed! I went to bed early, but I was so excited about the milk run, I couldn't sleep. I kept turning over and over and over in bed until the sheets wrapped me up like a mummy. I was still wide awake when Lily came to bed, then I woke up earlier than usual because I was still excited. When it finally came time for the milk run I was feeling pretty ~~siked psiked~~ psyked (I think that's how to spell it).

Getting on and off the truck was pretty tricky. As the milk truck arrived, it *sort of* slowed down, and we had to run to catch up then grab on to the handrail thingy and leap up on the ledge at the back. The ledge is where we stand when the truck is moving. Lenny went first and made it look easy. Then it was my turn and I had no trouble running along behind the truck coz it was going quite slow, but I didn't know there was such a knack in jumping onto the ledge. I grabbed the handrail okay, but didn't realise I needed to keep running in order to jump up on. Lenny could see what was happening straightaway and yelled, "Don't let go!" My feet started to drag along the road but before I knew it Lenny had pulled me up.

The others laughed, but Lenny said, "Don't worry, that happens to all of us the first time. You won't do it again."

I did do it again, 2 more times! It took a while for me to figure out how to get on and off something that's moving. I have a few grazes along my ankle bones to remind me. I did my milk run with a girl called Katrina—she's 16 and is really pretty. She showed me how to carry two full bottles in each hand.

There's a lot more to learn than I thought. You have to rotate the crates on the truck in the right order so that it makes room for the empties as you go. There are different coloured tokens for milk and cream and sometimes people want to buy tokens, so if you don't have any left in your pouch, you have to remember who it was and tell the driver so he can go back and sort it. The crates are heavy as anything, but I tried to make it look like it was easy for me. Katrina was telling me that when she started last year, milk was 4 cents a bottle, but in February it went up to 8 cents a bottle.

"Woah! That's double the price," I said.

"Yeah, people were pretty annoyed. Some even stopped us at the gate to complain about it," said Katrina.

I hope the price of my boots doesn't double before I buy them. I had to do a LOT of running with the milk trolley and it was really hard on some of the hills. I made sure I smiled and talked to the others though, so they wouldn't think I was finding it hard.

I was glad when we finished and got to go home, I was so hungry I had 2 extra bits of bread after tea. Now I see why Lenny is always so hungry after work. It was fun, but it was hard work too. I'm working every day this week. Yay! $$$$$$$$

MONDAY, 26 July

When I stepped out of bed this morning every muscle in my legs, bum, and arms hurt. All I seemed to say was, "Ow ow ouch ow." Mum said maybe the milk run was a bit too much for me. Luckily, Lenny jumped in and said everyone gets stiff and sore when they start out. He said it would wear off in a day or two. I stopped saying ouch after that, even though it hurt like crazy every time I moved. I had to bike to school today too, so I would be home in time for the milk run. I think that helped loosen my muscles by the time I got to school.

Once I got there, I talked to Charlotte about Tigi and the crew. She said they left on Saturday afternoon and her mum had gone back with them. Reckons she's okay with it because her mum is coming back for Christmas. But that's ages away! I don't know how she copes with that. She told me that Lenny had been at their place, hanging out with Rawiri and Tigi. I knew it! She reckons they are thinking about becoming Polynesian Panthers. Geeeezzzz!

Day 2 of the milk run was better. I got on the moving truck first time every time. Katrina showed me how to pick up 4 empties all at once. She's really good at moving full and empty bottles quickly, and I tried really hard to keep up with her. She told me to keep the full crates of milk at the back of my trolley and the empties at the front, but I forgot and found out why you do that. If there is too much weight at the front the trolley can topple over, which is what happened to me when I hit a curb. The crates sort of slipped off but luckily the bottles stayed in them and none got broken, thank goodness.

I'd never thought about how much was involved with a milk run before. I'm learning loads of new things. I get a free bottle of milk a day as well now, so Mum made us all hot milk Milos after tea. It was yummy, the only thing I hated was the skin on the top of it.

SATURDAY, 31 July

Mum let me sleep in, and I didn't wake up till 11:30. She said she knew I was tired when I'd fallen asleep watching, *Donny & Marie*. I remember them singing "Puppy Love" and next thing I knew, Dad was waking me up and telling me to go to bed.

There are 2 bits of good news from today. First, I'm keeping my milk run. Hip-hip-hooray! Lenny said our driver told Mr. Walker (the owner of the milk run) that I was a great worker, that I'd picked things up quickly, and I was strong for such a young girl. And although you'd think that's the best news of the day, then I found out I'm getting paid for all the work I've done already!

I didn't know people got paid when they were on a trial. I'm so happy right now. Lenny said I'll get paid on Tuesday. I don't know how much I'll get. I'm gonna get a jar and put it in my undies drawer and keep all of my money in it. I asked Mum how much people usually get paid. She said the minimum wage is $1.95 an hour but I won't get paid that much because I'm a kid. I don't really care how much it is, I'm just excited to be earning money. I guess the Māori designs I put on my rakau have brought me good fortune. I didn't know designs could be so powerful. I'll have to tell Mr. Parker about that when I see him.

I've got a day off my milk run tomorrow. I don't feel like I need a day off, but we all get one day off a week. I think I'm getting used to pushing the trolley up and down the hills as it seemed a bit easier today.

I'm on ironing duty at home now that I have a milk run, coz I'm not there at teatime to help with the dishes anymore.

I bet I dream of jars full of money tonight!

SUNDAY, 1 August

Did the ironing today, and it took ages! I hate ironing shirts, I should have kept the tea towels and hankies till last coz they're easiest to do. Next time I'll do that. Mum said I should iron while I'm watching the Disney movie coz work seems to go quicker when you're watching TV, so next time I'll do that as well.

MONDAY, 2 August

On the back of the milk truck, as we were heading home today, I asked Lenny if he'd been hanging out with Rawiri. He said he had, which I already knew from Charlotte. He said they talked a lot about Tigi and how the Polynesian Panthers have been protesting the dawn raids.

About a month ago (just near my birthday) the Panthers were called to their headquarters in Auckland. Flippin' heck! They have headquarters? It's like a real-life *Get Smart* series. I wonder if there's a secret door to get in?

The Panthers were told there was going to be a demo (that's a protest, I think) and they had a mission. Apparently, some of their supporters are university students and they came up with an idea to do a dawn raid on some politicians! Each group was given the address of a politician, a megaphone, and spotlights. Then, at 3 o'clock in the morning, each carload went to a different politician's house. Tigi was in a car with some pālagi (white people) from other groups who are also fighting injustice. Tigi told Lenny and Rawiri they knew it was illegal, but they also knew it was the right thing to do. He said they were organised and well prepared and were glad to have people from other groups supporting them, and lucky to have university students coming up with fresh ways to protest. Maybe Dad was right about a university education being important.

Tigi's group got the house of a politician called Bill Birch. When they pulled up, it was cold and foggy and everything was quiet. (It sounded like a great setting for a scary story.) They shone the spotlights on the house and called over the megaphone, "Bill Birch—come out and show us your passport," and other stuff like that. When the lights went on in the house, everyone jumped back in the car and sped away so they wouldn't get caught. Tigi said he knew it had worked when he heard one of the politicians interviewed on the radio next day, saying, "How dare these people come to our houses at such an ungodly hour!"

Excuse me! How do they think Pacific Islanders feel when the government does that to them? Exactly. The whole point was to show them how it felt—and now they know. He said that's when the Panthers knew they had succeeded, but Tigi said it didn't have as much effect as they'd hoped, because of bias in the media.

I don't really get that. I thought the media just reported the news, but Lenny told me that the media can influence public opinion by choosing <u>what</u> they report and <u>how</u>, and that's why loads of people don't actually know how bad things are for the Islanders. That made me mad because it seems really unfair. Sounds like another civil rights problem to me. I can't believe how brave Tigi and the other Panthers are. Lenny said if he was there he would have done it too. I would've been really worried if Lenny was with them.

TUESDAY, 3 August

PAY DAY—WOWEEEEE! I got paid $8.40. I can't believe it! I'm so rich! It will only take me 2 weeks to buy my boots. I get 70 cents an hour, and I do 2 hours a day for 6 days a week. My pay came in a small brown envelope with my name on it. Since this is my very first pay packet ever, I kept the envelope. I was thinking of buying some jeans but I can't decide if I want Levi's or

Wranglers. I also saw these FAB bib overalls in pre-washed denim—they're the coolest!

I got a coffee jar and put all my money in it, then got it out and laid it out on my bed 4 times. Lily told me to stop playing with it or I'll wear it out.

I want to spend a bit . . . I think I'll buy some Milkybars and Big Charlie bubblegum tomorrow.

WEDNESDAY, 4 August

The cultural food day at school will be on the 20th of August, the last day of the term. Mr. Parker is going to put down a hāngi as part of it. They need family members to help—men to help put the hāngi down and ladies to help peel veges and serve the food. I asked Mum and Dad if they could come. They're thinking about it. I still have to decide what to make for it. Not cornbeef stew, that's for sure. I don't want to start another fight, although I think me and Charlotte are all good now.

After the milk run I biked to the shop and got some treats. I got a Nut Roll each for Mum and Dad, Milkybars for all us kids, and some Big Charlies just for me, which I put in my jersey drawer so my little brothers won't find them. Everyone was pleased with my treats, and I felt good doing something nice for the family with my own money. I spent $1.30. Archie was at our place, so I gave him my Milkybar and I had a Big Charlie.

Dad said it was good to be generous to others. Mum said I should think about setting some goals and saving some of my money. She said I should have some small goals, like the boots, and some bigger goals, like they did when they bought our colour TV. Maybe my big goal will be a pair of boots in every colour. I'm going to ask Mum and Dad if I can shout dinner for the family. I remember Lenny doing that when he first got his milk run.

THURSDAY, 5 August

Mum and Dad said I can shout tea tomorrow night. It's Thursday so there's late-night shopping, and after my milk run, Mum will take me to Porirua shopping centre. I'm going to shout us hot chicken with bread and butter to make chicken sandwiches. YUM!

FRIDAY, 6 August

Hot chooks are the best. I brought 2 of them so there was plenty for everyone. It cost $2.50 per chicken, 32c for the butter, 16c per loaf of bread (I got 2), so altogether it cost $5.64. So far, I have spent $6.94 of my pay and have $1.46 left, so I'll put that aside for my boots. It might take a few weeks to save for them. When I went to pay for the food, the checkout girl said, "Hey, I love your purse," meaning my coffee jar. I felt a bit embarrassed, so actually I think I'll buy a purse next.

Ethan's a blimmin' pest! He wrote this. The little scuzz bucket better hope I don't tell on him or he'll be in so much trouble. I shouldn't have left my diary lying around. He better not be reading it—or else!!!!!!! You got that, Ethan Savea??

SATURDAY, 7 August

Uh-oh. Ethan nearly got Mum and Dad in trouble. There was a knock on the door this morning and it was the TV licence people. They check all the houses because it's hard to know if people have a TV because sometimes they don't have an outside aerial, they just have rabbit ears. Anyway, the lady was asking Mum questions about our TV and Mum knew we only had a licence for a black and white set because the colour licence costs too much. When the lady asked if our TV was black and white or colour, Mum said black and white. Ethan was listening and piped up with, "Hey, Mum, does the colour TV in the lounge not count?"

I think the TV lady knew what was going on but she never said anything, she just gave Mum a pamphlet with the licencing rules and left. Ethan got a big telling-off for butting into adult conversations, but at least he didn't cry this time.

MONDAY, 9 August

We found out today that the speech competition is on Saturday the 13 of November. No set topic, it's free choice. First prize for my age group is $25 plus a $10 book token. Wow, that's a massive prize! I'm going to try really hard with my speech. At lunchtime, Mr. Carter worked with those of us who are entered in the competition. I'm representing our school in the 13 to 14 age group. Lucky I've had my birthday, coz I just made it into that group. Actually, maybe it's not lucky. If I was in the 11 to 12 group, I might have a better chance.

Mr. Carter gave us some tips for preparing our speeches. He said to think of something that will be interesting to people of all ages. Maybe I should ask Alice if I can use her "Man on the Moon" topic, I'm sure everyone would find that interesting. Mr. Carter also said we should know our topic VERY well and that we should have a strong interest in it ourselves. Hmmm, maybe the "Man on the Moon" isn't for me after all. My last speech was about myself, so I knew that topic well, but I don't think it would be interesting to people who don't know me. I reckon I could do fun facts about Donny and Marie Osmond—everyone would be into that. I'll have to think about this a bit more. Mr. Carter is going to keep checking on us to see how we're doing. I know it's a few months away yet, but I'm already starting to feel worried.

TUESDAY, 10 August

Yippeee, PAYDAY again! Another $8.40, so now I have $9.86 in my coffee jar. I'm not going to spend anything this week. I was talking to Katrina while we were standing on the back of the milk truck. She told me she spent all her first month's pay, then her mum made her start saving some each week, and now she has over $100 in her bank. Flippin' heck!!!!!! She said now that she's saved so much, she wants to keep going so she can buy a car when she gets her licence. Katrina's been doing the milk run for almost a year now. If I start saving like her, I'll be able to buy whatever I want. It's so exciting having a job and some money.

I asked Katrina if she's Samoan, coz she's brown too. She said she's Rarotongan but lots of people think she's either Samoan or Māori. I asked if Rarotonga is the same as Tonga but she said they're different places in the Pacific Islands. I asked her if she knew about the dawn raids on Pacific Islanders. She didn't, and I don't think she was interested—she started talking about some flared jeans she was thinking of buying from James Smith's. She said her mum helps her put things like clothes on lay-by, and then she pays them off over a couple of months. When you've finished paying it off,

you get the clothes or whatever that you put on lay-by. I didn't know about lay-bys, but Katrina said it's a great way to make sure you don't miss out on stuff you really, really want in case it's sold out by the time you've saved up the money. This is the best news ever.

After I ate my tea, I asked Mum if she would help me lay-by my boots. She said it would be better to just save the money and I said, "But what if I miss out on them?" She's thinking about it.

WEDNESDAY, 11 August

It was Mr. Parker day again today. He told us we need to know who is available for the hāngi next week. Whoops, I'd forgotten to check with Mum and Dad, so I asked them tonight. They'd forgotten too. Mum said she'll be fine coz it's during the day, but Dad will need to see if he can get the day off. Mr. Parker had written the details on the blackboard and we copied them.

Thursday 19th

3:00–5:00 p.m.

Ladies—vegetable preparation, make stuffing

Men—dig hāngi pit, collect rocks and baskets (we need someone with a trailer)

Friday 20th

5:00 a.m. Men light the fire, and put the hāngi down around 6:30 a.m.

11:00 a.m. Ladies prepare tables

12:00 p.m. Men lift the hāngi

12:30 p.m. Ladies serve the hāngi

Colin said his dad has a trailer we can use. Mr. Morrison is going to ring him. Mr. Parker said we could do the songs we've been learning to thank our parents for their help. He said we can also do the rakau routines to entertain everyone while they're eating. FUN!!!

We practised our songs, and everyone seemed to sing better today.

THURSDAY, 12 August

Yay, Dad can help out with the hāngi. He took an annual leave day, which is a big deal coz he's taking 2 weeks' leave when we go to Auckland to see Grandma and Grandpa. Dad's keen to learn how to put down a hāngi. He told us he knows how to do an umu (the Samoan version) but he's never done one for us. He said an umu is cooked on top of the ground whereas a hāngi is cooked **in** the ground. Ewww, I hope we don't get any dirt in our food! Dad said hāngi food is beautiful. I can't wait, and I'm looking forward to showing off the songs and the rakau routines we've been doing.

FRIDAY, 13 August

Everyone reckons Friday the 13th is bad luck. I thought it was rubbish until I slipped while I was getting on the milk truck tonight. I was still holding the handrail, so I got dragged along the road a bit until Lenny yelled at Richard (the driver) to stop. I ripped my pants and grazed my leg really badly. Richard took me home to get it cleaned up and said I should stay there, which Mum and Dad agreed with. I didn't want to, but Mum said I've been working hard and needed a rest. Richard said I should have Saturday off as well. I am so annoyed. That's 2 days of pay I'm going to miss out on—$2.80 less in my pay next week.

SATURDAY, 14 August

I went with Mum to get groceries. I still felt stink about missing 2 days of work so I took my money jar and bought a purse to cheer me up. I got this cool green and blue beaded one, then I saw a matching shoulder bag and I couldn't help myself—I had to have it as well. Blast it, I spent more than I meant to and now I only have $2.36 left! I think lay-by is the only way I can get the boots now. I talked to Mum about it again and she said that it would be okay but I needed to have 20 percent of the whole price for the first lay-by payment. The boots are $12.97, so I need $2.59 for the first payment. I don't have enough for that so I'll have to wait till Tuesday before I can do a lay-by. Blow, I shouldn't have bought the shoulder bag but I didn't know about the 20 percent thing. I could ask Mum for a loan of 23c, but I've only had 2 paydays and I don't think she'd be impressed with me asking for a loan already. I'll just wait until Tuesday, then have I'll have heaps for the lay-by. I'll be getting less pay next week so I need to be careful with my money.

SUNDAY, 15 August

The Disney movie tonight was *The Love Bug* about this cool little VW car, called Herbie, that does stuff all by himself! Ethan and Tavita nearly wet themselves laughing, it was pretty funny. Mum was kind and did the ironing tonight. It was nice to have a break and just watch TV.

Lenny told me Charlotte has started on the milk run and she filled in for me on Saturday. OH NO! I hope I don't lose my job. They must think it's okay to take on 13-year-olds now since I showed them what a good worker I was.

MONDAY, 16 August

I talked to Charlotte about the milk run today. She thinks it's really hard work, but she liked it. She's going to work this week to learn some more, then she'll be the on-call person to fill in if someone is sick or away. PHEW! Thank goodness my job is safe. I'll make sure I concentrate from now on when I'm getting on and off the truck.

TUESDAY, 17 August

Mr. Morrison played the guitar today and we went through the songs for the cultural food day. I love singing them. We worked out who is doing what for the rakau, the whole class is doing what Mr. Parker taught us and then me, Tania, Colin, Walter, and Jonathan are doing our made-up routine. Mr. Morrison let us practise for some of the afternoon.

We also made a class list of what food people are bringing. Mum, Dad, and I are bringing chop suey, which Dad's making. There are tons of parents coming to help. I think they're all keen to have some hāngi.

I worked with Charlotte on the milk run tonight. She asked me lots of questions about tokens and stuff and said I was really fast at moving bottles around. I thought she did a pretty good job too. She kept up with the running and we took turns pushing the trolley.

I asked her what she was bringing for the cultural lunch. (Can you believe we were having a conversation about the very thing we had our fight over?) She said a hāngi is from her culture so her auntie is giving some veges to go into it. I hadn't thought about where the food for the hāngi was coming from. Charlotte said the school was providing the meat, and the veges and stuffing were split between some of the families in the class. Seems a good idea.

WEDNESDAY, 18 August

It was Colin's birthday today so when Mr. Parker came in he taught us to sing "Happy Birthday" in Māori. Anyone else would be embarrassed to have the class sing to them, but not Colin. He loved it, he even started conducting us. Mr. Parker called Colin a hard case.

Mr. Parker drew a diagram of the hāngi on the blackboard, like this:

He's funny, he actually drew the happy men too. He said they're happy because everything was done right for the hāngi and that is very important. We learnt that some jobs are especially for men and some are for women, and there are things like prayers (karakia) that need to happen first. He reminded us to tell our parents about the preparation tomorrow afternoon. I told him Dad couldn't come tomorrow, but he'd be there on Friday morning at 5:00 a.m.

He reminded us to all bring our own plates and cutlery— I must remember to tell Mum and Dad about that.

THURSDAY, 19 August

Preparation day for the hāngi was neat. We spent the afternoon clearing the classroom and getting set up for tomorrow, then we practised our songs and stuff. Mum picked up the boys early so she could be there at 3 o'clock for the preparation. She ended up being in charge of the kitchen so we got to go into the staff room to see her. The ladies made the stuffing and peeled the veges and put them in big tubs of water. The men dug the hole and got all the firewood, rocks, and sacks ready for the morning.

It's been such a busy week, I forgot all about the lay-by for my boots. Tomorrow I'll ask Mum if we can go to the shops when I finish work.

SATURDAY, 21 August

We never got to the shops yesterday, but Mum said we can go today, THANK GOODNESS!

The cultural food day was good. Dad loved learning about the hāngi. He said Mr. Parker said a karakia, then they dug a hole big enough for all the food baskets. They made a fire beside the hole and spread the hāngi stones through it to heat up. They have to use special stones— volcanic rock—so they don't explode at high temperatures. (Wow, I didn't know there was so much to know about putting down a hāngi.) Then they burn the wood and rocks for hours to get the rocks super-duper hot. Dad said in the end they were glowing white. I thought that sounded wrong, and they should be glowing red, but he told us that when they are white they are about as hot as they can be.

Then they had to work quickly to get the rocks in the pit and place the food baskets on top. The baskets were lined with cabbage leaves and the meat was put in first. Then on top of the meat went the veges (potatoes, kumara, pumpkin, etc.), which were in mutton bags that had been soaking in water. Finally, the stuffing and more cabbage leaves were put on top in more mutton bags. Over top of the lot they put a sheet, which had also been soaked in water, to keep all the food clean. Dad told us that it had to be a sheet that had never been slept in because that is the right tikanga (Māori rules).

Mum thought it was a waste to use a perfectly good, brand-new sheet, but Dad said, "That's just the right way to do things, love." Over top of the sheet were laid mutton bags and sacks that had been soaking in water to make the steam. When everything was in place they finally piled the dirt on top, being careful to cover every part of it so that the steam didn't escape.

Once the hāngi was down they sat around drinking coffee and chatting. Mr. Parker asked loads of questions about putting down an umu, so Dad said he would teach him one day.

Lily saw Dad at morning teatime when he was walking from the staff room to our class and stopped to talk with him for a bit. Some girls from her class came over and asked if Dad was her boyfriend. Dad laughed, but Lily was horrified and told them it was her dad and not to be so silly. The girls told Lily she should be glad she has such a young, good-looking dad.

Eww, that's not cool! They shouldn't be saying things like that about our dad!

At 11:00 a.m. Mr. Morrison and Mr. Parker gave a speech to the parents and then said we should do our songs and rakau. Mr. Arbuckle our principal had come to watch as well. Our rakau group went first because we had our special performance to do. Colin got up to introduce us (of course), and he said, "Sofia's dad made these wooden rakau for our group and we've been practising almost every day." Dad smiled and looked proud. Then Colin said, "Sometimes we even add our own sound effects, but I don't think we will be doing that today . . ." Colin, Walter, and Jonathan laughed but I went bright red. WHAT THE HECK, COLIN BAKER?!

I don't think anyone realised what he was talking about, but I don't care, he should never have said that. Boys can be so dumb sometimes. Dad asked me later what Colin meant, but I said I had no idea. I think Dad knew I did—the whole room must have lit up with my bright red face.

After our performance, the whole class sang some songs. The singing was amazing! I think the whole school would have heard us. The parents clapped heaps.

When the hāngi came up, the ladies were busy putting it all out and making sure all the other food was heated and ready too. Mr. Parker said a karakia for the food and then it was time to eat. The parents, teachers, and Mr. Arbuckle went first, then the girls, then the boys and Mr. Morrison and Mr. Parker. I had some hāngi. It tasted kind of smoky, but I liked it. I also had one of Colin's cheese rolls, some chop suey (of course), and a yummy casserole that Tania's mum had made, it had sultanas in it. Mr. Parker told Dad the chop suey was the best he'd ever had. Dad said, "I'll make it again when you come to learn how to put an umu down."

"That's a deal," said Mr. Parker.

SUNDAY, 22 August

I am **SO** miserable!!!!!!!!

We finally went to lay-by my boots yesterday—and there weren't any in my size! I almost cried when the lady told us. I tried on a smaller size but hadn't even started to do up the laces and they were hurting like crazy. The lady said, "Well, they have been popular." That didn't help at all. I was sitting there with my big Island feet, feeling like an ugly sister from Cinderella, and that's all she could say. Mum asked if any of their other stores might have my size, and the lady said she would phone around and see, but she couldn't promise anything and we might have to pay extra to get them there.

WHAT? Obviously she doesn't know I'm paying for these with my own milk-run money. Actually, she wouldn't know that because Mum was doing the lay-by in her name. Oh well, I won't know until next week. Bummer. I went into Woolworth's and got some pick-n-mix lollies. I know I shouldn't have spent any money but I don't think I'll need it for my boots now. I spent too much and the pick-n-mix cost $1.13.

There was tons of ironing to do when we got home, and even the Disney movie was stink tonight.

I hope I can get my boots. Please, please, please! Fingers and toes crossed.

I forgot it's school holidays now. At least I can sleep in tomorrow.

TUESDAY, 24 August

It's payday, so now I have over $15 but we haven't heard about the boots yet so it doesn't really matter.

FRIDAY, 27 August

Tonight we all went to Porirua Centre for late-night shopping. I bought some View-Master reels from the magazine shop. They're cool. I got *I Dream of Jeannie*, a Countries of the World set about Greece, and a Peter Pan set. I let Ethan and Tavita look at the Peter Pan set. In one of the pictures it looks like the crocodile is coming right out of the picture at you, they loved it. The reels were $1.25 a set. Then we went to James Smith's and I saw this AMAZING COOLEST EVER halter-neck top. It was only $4.50 so I decided to get it. The colour is called burnt orange, pretty cool, eh. I thought it would be nice to buy something for Mum and Dad since they helped out so much at the cultural food day last week, so I got Mum a hand cream and some hankies for Dad. They were stoked.

When we watched *Donny & Marie*, I felt miserable all over again because she was wearing bright blue go-go boots. I was thinking, Boohoohoohoo (that's me crying quietly to myself). Seeing the boots must have jogged Mum's memory and she said, "Oh, I forgot to tell you, the lady from the shoe shop rang and they've got some boots for you—they'll be here next week."

I leapt off the couch and said, "Aw, Mum! Why didn't you tell me before we went to the shops? Now I've spent some of my money!"

"Sofia Christina Savea, do not raise your voice at me!" I didn't even know I was shouting, but I was so annoyed, I said (or shouted), "But, Mum, you know I wanted to lay-by them and now I've spent some more of my money."

Dad stepped in then and said, "Sofia," in a low, warning voice.

I stormed off to my room. I quickly counted my money—all I have left is $2.53. What is wrong with me? I keep spending all my money. I never thought earning money could cause me so much worry.

SUNDAY, 29 August

Uncle Joe rang today, and then I heard Dad and Mum talking about sending money to help pay for Grandma and Grandpa's trip to Auckland. Mum wasn't very happy about it. "We're already sending so much, do we have to?"

"That's just the way it is, Mary."

This time it was Mum's turn to raise her voice and storm off to her room. Dad went out and dug the garden.

I painted my toenails and tried on my new top. Lily came in and said, "Fab top. A pair of Wrangler jeans would go great with it."

I like that idea. I'll have to see how much they are. Whoops . . . there I go, spending my money again.

Dad made Mum a cup of tea and then he cooked a scrummy chow mein for dinner. I think he was trying to make up with Mum.

I told Lily and Lenny what happened and Lily said we should all give some of our money to help get Grandma and Grandpa to Auckland. I like the idea . . . but am worried I won't be able to get my boots.

MONDAY, 30 August

The first week of the holidays went so quick. During term time I can never wake up, so I thought I would sleep in every day, but instead I wake up early. It's payday tomorrow so I'll be able to do the lay-by.

WEDNESDAY, 1 September

Before Mum got home from work I hung the washing out, tidied up the bench, and got a cup of tea ready for her. I asked if she could take me to do the lay-by and she did.

I tried the boots on and didn't want to take them off. When the lady opened the box and pulled the tissue paper back, I must've been holding my breath because I let out a little gasp, Mum and the shop lady giggled a bit. It felt so good to know they are finally going to be mine. I ended up putting $3.00 on the lay-by so I could keep some to give Dad towards getting Grandma and Grandpa to Auckland. Mum said I should put more on, but I told her I want to keep some because I might go to the pictures with Lily.

Katrina's away on holiday, so Charlotte was on the milk run. I told her about the boots and she can't wait to see them. She told me Lenny has been spending heaps of

time at their place and she thinks he and Rawiri are up to something.

"Like what?" I asked.

She wasn't sure, but said the two of them would be talking away quietly, then whenever she came into the room she could tell they'd changed the subject. There was a meeting at their house last week and some of the people who were at the meeting with Tigi came, including Mr. Parker and Mr. Morrison. I really want to know what's going on now.

THURSDAY, 2 September

Me and the others put our money together to give to Dad. Lenny must have used heaps of his because I put $6, Lily put $8, but altogether we gave Dad $63.

I hadn't thought about how it would make Dad feel, but when we presented it to him tonight, he was obviously shocked as he didn't say anything for ages. He just sat there, tapping the arm of his chair. That's when I realised he was trying not to cry. When he did speak, his voice was really wavery and it was hard to hear him. All he said was, "Thank you, son, thank you, girls," then Mum got her hanky out and started dabbing her eyes.

We all sat there like statues for a bit, then Lenny said, "Hey, Dad, we're a team."

And I said, "Are we the kind of team that eats dough-nuts for supper?"

Everyone laughed, then Mum said, "How about some pikelets?"

FRIDAY, 3 September

Charlotte has found out what the boys are up to. They are planning a protest at Parliament!

"NO WAY!" I said. "Dad will kill Lenny if he finds out."

She told me they're protesting about an ad that was on TV last year as part of Muldoon's election campaign.

I thought, Wha-a-at? That doesn't sound like something worth protesting about. Charlotte didn't get it either. I'll have to ask Lenny what's going on. Charlotte thinks the protest is going to be next week. Oh boy, I hope there's not going to be trouble in our house because of this.

Only one more week of holidays, BOOHOO. Oh well, at least we have another holiday coming up in October, I can't wait to go to Auckland and see everyone again.

SATURDAY, 4 September

A fire engine came to our house today!

Mum and Dad went out early to the plant shop and us kids all stayed home. When they got back there was a fire engine and firemen on our front lawn. No prizes for guessing who was responsible . . . Dumbo #1, Ethan, and Dumbo #2, Tavita. When they got up, they decided to make homemade chips for breakfast. They peeled and sliced the spuds and put a heap of dripping fat in a pot on the stove to heat up. Then they went out to play cricket.

Me, Lily, and Lenny were still in bed. Next thing there was smoke pouring out the kitchen door and Mr. Wallace, our neighbour, was in our kitchen saving the day while Mrs. Wallace called the fire brigade. Once the boys realised what was happening, they hid under the house.

Mum and Dad got a heck of a fright to find a fire engine, some firemen, and the neighbours on the front lawn with us big kids, but Ethan and Tavita nowhere to be found. Lenny worked out where they would be and brought them out—bawling AGAIN! They were banished to sit on the back doorstep for ages after that.

Mum and Dad got a bit of a telling-off from the fire chief guy for leaving the kids unsupervised with hot dripping. Lenny started to argue with Mr. Fire Chief but Dad told him to leave it. Lenny was right though—Mum and Dad left us in charge but we didn't know the stupid boys would do that. I wonder if all little brothers are as dumb as mine.

Dad said they could've burnt the house down or, even worse, killed us, so we shut up after that. Mum had to wash the kitchen curtains and made the boys scrub the pot, but I think it'll have to be thrown out—it's very burnt.

At least we didn't have to take anyone to the hospital this time, thank goodness.

I think I've found out when the protest is going to be, coz I heard Lenny ask if he could have next Friday off the milk run. I asked him why, but he pretended not to hear and when the truck slowed down, he jumped off the back and got in the cab.

I'm a bit worried about all of this.

SUNDAY, 5 September

I was up early so did the ironing this morning. Mum washed some sheets and put them on the line and when I looked out the window, Ethan and Tavita had opened out the sheets and were leaning into the pocket of them. They call it their upside-down tent. They keep their feet on the ground and run in circles around the clothesline. When they're going fast enough they lift their feet and it's like flying.

I remembered doing that when I was younger too, so I went out to have a look and ended up having a go. It was great fun but I was too heavy and the pegs kept popping off the line. I should've known this was a bad sign, because, next thing I knew, the clothesline was on a real lean and my scumbag brothers were inside telling on me.

Mum came out and said, "Sofia, you should know better."

Fortunately, Dad and Lenny managed to fix the clothesline. Mum was right—I should know better ... better than to trust those boys! Telltale-tits.

WEDNESDAY, 8 September

Lily and I caught the bus to Porirua shopping centre today. Mum gave me the lay-by card and I put another $4 on the boots. Only $5.97 to go, yippee!

We looked at heaps of clothes and I tried on some jeans and some bib overalls. Lily tried on a poncho, it was cool. We didn't have enough money to buy them so we thought we could ask Mum to do another lay-by for us. Mum said to me, "One lay-by at a time is enough." She said Lily could do one for her poncho, but that she should think about it for a week or so to decide if she really wants it.

Afterwards, I told Lily I think Mum's wrong and she shouldn't wait, coz that's how I nearly missed out on my boots. Lily said she thought Mum had a fair point, which made me wonder if Lily does really want the poncho, after all.

SUNDAY, 12 September

WOWEEEE, it's been full on around here.

So . . . Lenny had the day off the milk run on Friday for the protest . . . but then he had Saturday off too, because he got arrested and taken to the police cells! Dad had to go get him. It sounds really bad, which it was for a bit, but it ended up good coz Mr. Morrison and Mr. Parker were arrested too (that's not the good part). They ended up coming to see Dad last night to explain what was going on. I thought Dad would be angry with them, but I know he likes them both and when they explained, he was really good about it all.

Charlotte was right, the protest was about a TV ad from last year. Mr. Muldoon (who wanted to be Prime Minister) got Hanna-Barbera (who make Scooby-Doo and stuff like that) to make a cartoon for his election campaign. The ad showed a person with an Afro and brown skin fighting with a Pākehā person and the cartoon was saying that people are coming in from other places and now there aren't enough jobs to go around.

Mr. Morrison and Mr. Parker told Dad this is just one example of racism in New Zealand, where the government is targeting Pacific Islanders. They said it's true that there are lots of overstayers, but only a third of them are from the Pacific Islands—which means two-thirds are not. Dad asked where the others were from, and they said places like Australia and countries in Europe.

That's when Dad finally got it. "So Mr. Muldoon's TV ad is blaming Pacific Islanders for the problem?"

"Exactly, Sid, that's what makes it racist because they're only targeting Pacific Islanders as the problem, when in fact there are a lot of different nationalities that make up overstayers." Mr. Morrison went on to tell Dad a bit about the Polynesian Panthers and how they've helped Pacific Islanders to know their rights.

Mr. Parker said to Dad, "I'm not telling you what to think, Siaosi, but I would be proud to have a son like

Lenny who is prepared to stand up for the rights of others."

Dad thanked them both for coming over and said it has given him a lot to think about. I liked that Mr. Parker used Dad's real name.

Lily and I sat on Lenny's bed and he told us what happened at the protest. There were about 20 people, and some of them chained themselves to pillars on the steps of Parliament and used a megaphone to chant their messages about stopping the dawn raids and racist government ads. When the police came and asked them to leave, the protesters said things like, "We have the right to protest peacefully, we have the right to have our say."

The police had to use bolt cutters for the chains, which was when a fight broke out between them and the protesters. That was why the boys got taken to the police cells—because of the fight. Lenny said they were provoked because the police used batons on them and pushed their faces into the ground when they weren't even fighting. I asked Lenny how it felt to be a protester. He said he felt really excited when they set up the protest, but scared when it was actually happening. He was worried about getting arrested, mostly because of how

Dad would react. It was great that Mr. Morrison and Mr. Parker were with him as they told him they'd come and talk with Dad, which they did.

MONDAY, 13 September

Lenny was on the news tonight! There was just a quick shot showing him with the protesters and the police taking him away. The news report made it sound like they were just a bunch of deadbeat, long-haired trouble-makers. Lenny was angry because they never showed the part where Rawiri was interviewed. He said Rawiri had said some great stuff about what they were protesting, but the news reporters didn't show any of it.

"You see, Dad," Lenny said, "the Muldoon government has been convincing the public that Pacific Islanders are the problem. The government's been trying to keep the dawn raids quiet, and sometimes the newsmakers help them. In Auckland, the cops did a blitz on the streets looking for overstayers—they stopped more than a thousand Polynesian-looking people—men, women, anyone with brown skin. Out of that thousand, they caught just twenty overstayers."

Dad just made a tutting sound and shook his head. Then he asked some more questions about it and Lenny said the news media are supporting this all over the country.

One newspaper, *The Southland Times* in Invercargill, reported that "if you support these illegal immigrants, you could be keeping New Zealanders out of jobs." Lenny said the problem is that all the media attention only shows Polynesian people as the overstayers, so the general public naturally think that's the problem.

"Yeah, I've heard a few guys at work making remarks like that about Polynesians," Dad said.

"So ask them which job they applied for that a Polynesian got instead," Lenny told Dad.

Wow, Lenny and Dad talking like this is very cool. Both on the same side for a change.

Only 4 weeks till we go to Auckland!

TUESDAY, 14 September

We had a coaching session for the speech competition today. We have to come up with possible topics by next week. Mr. Carter said it doesn't matter what the topic is, it's about how you make people feel connected to the idea. He gave us some tips about how to do that with things like helping people get a picture in their head. That sounded a bit weird to me, but when Mr. Carter read us a couple of pieces of writing, I could see what he meant. He's a good teacher.

When he asked if anyone already had an idea for their speech, I mentioned Martin Luther King Jr. Mr. Carter asked why I chose him, which put me off a bit.

"I thought you might know why," I replied.

"I may well do—but I want you to explain it to me, and try to convince us both that it's a good topic." Man, he's clever at getting people to think.

The bad thing from today is that Charlotte told me Mr. Morrison might be in trouble with the school education board (I think that's what it's called) because of getting arrested on the protest. I hope not. When I told Lenny, he got really angry about it.

Payday today. I'll put another $3 on my lay-by and start saving the rest for when we go to Auckland.

WEDNESDAY, 15 September

Charlotte said Rawiri phoned Tigi and the Panthers to talk about the protests and getting arrested. The Panthers are talking with this young lawyer guy called David Lange, who might help to get the charges dropped against him, Lenny, Mr. Morrison, and Mr. Parker. This is great news. I hope he's a good lawyer. Charlotte said he's the man who helped the Panthers make legal aid booklets to give out to the Islanders.

THURSDAY, 16 September

Lenny got called into Mr. Arbuckle's office today to explain why he was involved in the protest. Mr. Arbuckle must've seen the news too. He asked Lenny lots of questions about his involvement—and about Mr. Morrison's too. Lenny told Mr. Arbuckle he should ask Mr. Morrison himself, which Mr. Arbuckle didn't much like.

Lenny didn't tell him much and Mr. Arbuckle said he didn't like his obstructive attitude and he would be talking with his parents. Sure enough, Mum got a phone call this afternoon. She and Dad have to go to see the principal on Monday. (Maybe they'll get a detention—hahahaha, just kidding.) Lenny doesn't think Mr. Arbuckle knows about the arrest, so I wonder what he'll do if he finds out about that.

MONDAY, 20 September

I don't know how, but Mr. Arbuckle <u>does</u> know about the arrest. He's talking about getting Lenny expelled from school. Mum and Dad were not pleased. More than anything, they want him to finish school and pass his University Entrance exams. Lenny told them about the Panthers' lawyer, so Dad went to Rawiri's to get a phone number to call them. Dad was amazing. He phoned the Panther headquarters and told them what was happening and they're looking into what can be done.

FRIDAY, 24 September

Everyone was so busy with Lenny's school problems that we never went to the shopping centre to pick up my lay-by.

The Panthers' lawyer, David Lange, told Dad to give his phone number to the principal, and when Dad did, he said it made Mr. Arbuckle do an about-face.

"Mr. Savea, there's no need to involve lawyers."

"Mr. Arbuckle, this is my son's education and his future depends on it so I will do whatever it takes to protect that."

Mr. Arbuckle mumbled some stuff about what a good student Lenny has been over the years and what promise he shows, and finally said he'll let him off—this time.

David Lange told Dad that the arrest charges will probably be dropped against all the protesters, because there are lots of reports from the public about the police provoking the protesters to get a reaction so they could arrest them.

Gee whiz, that guy David Lange seems to be a pretty good lawyer. Maybe they should make him Prime Minister instead of Mr. Muldoon.

Me and Lenny asked for time off work today for our trip to Auckland. That means Charlotte will get heaps of work while we're away.

SUNDAY, 26 September

We have to make toast on the stove with the cake cooler rack now because someone left the toaster cord lying across the element, not realising that Mum had turned the element on while she was getting the porridge ready. The cord burnt through and blew the toaster off the bench, as well as blowing all the fuses in the house.

It made such a loud explosion that everyone came running to see what had happened. Minty and Jaffa were asleep in the lounge and they got such a fright they took off, and Minty ran straight into the glass on the front door. Funny!

Ethan was crying and saying it wasn't him, and sur-prise, surprise, it turns out it wasn't this time—it was Lenny who did it. There you go—even big boys are stupid. Anyway, it's a real pain because you have to stand and wait for the toast to cook then turn it over and watch it so it doesn't burn. We don't want the fire engines here again.

TUESDAY, 28 September

Working with Mr Carter today, we had to share our possible topics. I freaked out coz I haven't done anything since last week. I thought about pretending I'd been sick, but in the end I just said, "Sorry, Mr. Carter, we've had a lot going on at home and I haven't thought about the speech."

I thought he'd be really cross, but instead he said, "Is there anything going on there that you could use as your topic?" which made me think that Mr. Carter must know all about what's been happening with Lenny, and that he agrees with it, otherwise he wouldn't have suggested that. I felt like a bit of a dummy. All I said was, "Ah, dunno." Mr. Carter told me to keep thinking about it and try to nut something out for next week.

Payday today. I haven't spent anything for the last two weeks. I'm so rich now, but I still need to pick up my boots.

SATURDAY, 2 October

Tried to work on my speech today but it didn't go very well. I thought about what Mr. Carter said and came up with these ideas:

1. What are the dawn raids?

2. Who are overstayers?

3. Who are the Polynesian Panthers and what do they do? (I thought this was the best one but I didn't manage to write anything down about them.)

I don't think I'll be in the speech competition after all.

SUNDAY, 3 October

The Disney movie tonight was called *Old Yeller*. It was s-o-o-o-o-o-o-o-o sad, I can't stop thinking about it. I wish I hadn't watched it now.

Dad made boiled chicken and rice risotto for tea. Yum. I could eat the whole pot of risotto on my own.

Only 7 days until we go to Auckland! Super-duper exciting!! It's good we're not leaving till Sunday morning because me and Lenny can do the milk run on Saturday.

MONDAY, 4 October

(From now on this will be known as the day of the big secret!)

Charlotte asked if I would take a present to Auckland for her mum. "It's not very big," she said, so I said okay. She told me, "The easiest place to take it is the Panthers' headquarters, right in town."

I said I'd need to check with Mum and Dad first to see if we can go there.

Charlotte said, "It'll be good for Mum to have a nice gift because it's a year since my dad left."

I didn't know what to say at first. I thought for a moment, then I said, "I'm really sorry your dad died."

Charlotte looked at me oddly and said, "He hasn't died."

I was so confused and said, "Yes he did. You told Mr. Arbuckle he was dead the day we had the fight."

She looked me straight in the eye and said, "Well, I lied."

I REALLY didn't know what to say then, I opened my mouth a few times but nothing came out. Charlotte looked at me and said, "Stop it, you look like a goldfish, opening and closing your mouth like that."

When I got myself together, I blurted out, "Why on earth would you lie to Mr. Arbuckle like that?"

What she told me next shocked me again. "My dad's in Tonga. He was an overstayer. He got deported a year ago."

I think I was doing the goldfish again because Charlotte paused and looked at me with her eyebrow raised. I just said, "Oh!"

"We were all living in Auckland but had to leave suddenly because Immigration were looking for Dad. So we came here to Porirua to stay with Mum's sister. They tracked us down here, and Dad had to go to jail for a few days. Then he was allowed to come home, but had to report to the police station every day. A month later, he was deported back to Tonga."

So many things were going through my head:

1. Charlotte's part Tongan! And there she was being mean to me about being Samoan?

2. Now I know why her mum is with the Panthers.

3. What will happen with her dad?

4. How did her dad come to be an overstayer?

5. I knew the dawn raids were real, but this confirms they're really real—and people do get taken away!

I should have asked about her dad but my mind was all over the show. Instead I blurted, "Craig doesn't sound like a Tongan surname." Geez I can be dumb sometimes. Like that mattered!

Charlotte didn't seem bothered. "Craig isn't Tongan. My dad's surname is Nuku. When we left Auckland we started using Mum's mother's name so the immigration people couldn't find us. My real name is Charlotte Nuku." She went on to explain, "I'm Tongan on dad's

133

side and Māori and Pākehā on my mum's side. Rawiri's mum and my mum are sisters."

Wow, this is becoming like a real-life spy story. "Will you see your dad again?"

Charlotte said she didn't know. Her dad had come to New Zealand in 1960 on a work permit thingy. He was supposed to go back when it expired, but he met her mum, had a family, and never went back. She said they'd heard that her dad's auntie dobbed him in so the police would leave her alone. What a cow! I didn't say that though. Charlotte's dad got a warning that something was up and they took off to Wellington to try and get the paperwork sorted, but it was too late.

I said to Charlotte, "Why didn't you just tell Mr. Arbuckle that?"

She raised her eyebrow again and said, "Well, Sofia, you and I had just had a fight and I didn't want you to know my business. Besides, I don't think Mr. Arbuckle would understand."

Now that I think about it, she was probably right, Mr. Arbuckle didn't get why Lenny was protesting, so I don't think he would get it about Charlotte's dad being an overstayer.

I asked why they didn't all go to Tonga with her dad and she said it was too expensive and her mum is working with the Panthers to try and get her dad back here.

Poor Charlotte! Poor Charlotte's mum! Poor Charlotte's dad!

I'm glad people are protesting about this.

TUESDAY, 5 October

Mr. Carter liked my topics. He said using a question for the title was an excellent idea. He showed me how to do a mind map to organise my ideas. It was good and I think it'll help me. I told Mr. Carter I'll be away for the next two weeks, so he told me just to keep working on it while I'm away and we'll look at it together when I get back.

People who overstayed their work visa
2/3rds AUS., U.S, EUROPE
1/3 PACIFIC

WHAT are the DAWN RAIDS?

Homes get raided by police looking for overstayers

Police are only raiding Pacific Islanders

Happens really early in the morning

People get dragged off to jail

WHO are ? OVERSTAYERS?

WHO are the POLYNESIAN PANTHERS?

I can take the present for Charlotte's mum. Dad said he wanted to go to the Panthers' headquarters anyway to thank them for helping with Lenny. This is exciting. I wonder if Tigi will be there with baby Che.

Payday again. I need to get Mum to take me to get my boots!!!!!!

FRIDAY, 8 October

We've been busy getting ready for the trip to Auckland. I didn't think Mum would take me to pay off my lay-by and get my boots, but she did. They're <u>SO</u> amazing. ♡ ♡ ♥ ♡

I put them on as soon as we got in the car and I am still wearing them. Dad reckons I'll probably sleep in them. Actually, I was thinking about it, I could dangle my feet out the end of the bed and then I would see them when I wake up. Haha.

I keep touching them, coz they're shiny and smooth and I love the feel of the metal clips. I'm supercalifragilisticexpialidocious happy. (I learnt to spell that when we had a class competition to find the longest word. The actual longest word was "antidisestablishmentarianism." No idea what it means, but mine wasn't counted as no one thought it was a real word.) Anyway, now I have my boots for Auckland. Hooray! I bet my cousins will love them too.

Rawiri is going to stay at our house (in Lenny's room) to look after the animals while we're away. I wonder if Lenny knows about Charlotte's dad being deported?

MONDAY, 11 October

Man, that was a long trip yesterday. We left at 9:00 a.m. and got to Uncle Joe's about 6:00 p.m. It was so squashy in the car. We started out with Mum, Dad, and Lenny in the front, and me, Lily, Ethan, and Tavita in the back. The Vauxhall Cresta is way bigger than our last car and the bench seat in the front means 3 people can fit okay. We were only allowed a pillow and one small bag each, so I wore my boots to make more room in my bag.

We stopped at Otaki for fresh hot bread, we haven't had that for ages. Mum got one loaf for the front seat and one for the back. Mmm, it was crusty on the outside and fluffy on the inside. We all picked pieces off and ate it. She got 2 more loaves to take to Uncle Joe's.

Half an hour later Ethan and Tavita were fighting, so Lenny got in the back and Ethan got put in the front. Lenny put Tavita on his knee so there was a bit more room.

We started singing and took turns picking the song. Tavita picked "Jingle Bells." Dad said it's a bit early for Christmas carols but Tavita carried on. Turns out he didn't really know the words. He was singing, "Jingle bells, jingle bells, jingle all the way, ho Mc fun it is to ride on a one tooth slopping sleigh, hey!"

We all laughed then joined in using Tavita's words and laughed some more. When we finished, Ethan said, "Tavita, you dummy, it's not a 'one tooth slopping sleigh,' it's a 'one horse open slave.'"

Hahahaha!

Dad nearly had to pull over he was laughing so much. That part of the trip was fun, the rest was long and hot and my feet were boiling in my boots. I slept for some of the trip. We stopped at Bulls for a stretch and Dad brought us all an ice cream. I got hokey-pokey. Mum told us when she was a kid they used to make their own hokey-pokey and it's really easy. She's going to teach us how to make it when we get back from Auckland. We stopped at Taupo for hot chips and then at a park in Hamilton so the kids could have a play.

By the time we got to Uncle Joe's, we were all tired and stiff, but as soon as we got out of the car and started hugging and kissing everyone we got full of energy again. Dad hugged Grandma and Grandpa for ages and they were all crying. I started to get tears in my eyes watching them, and then I saw that most of the grown-ups and some of the kids were crying too. It's been 6 years since Dad saw them.

After we unpacked, all the adults sat around talking. Lots of it was in Samoan so us kids went to the rooms. There are 18 of us staying at Uncle Joe's. Him and Auntie Aletta, and their 2 kids, Suzanne (Suz, she's my age, her middle name is Lily after Grandma as well) and Alofa (which means "love" in Samoan, which is pretty cool, she's 11). Us 3 and Lily are sleeping on mattresses behind the couch in the lounge, which is cool bananas.

Auntie Loretta (Dad's older sister) came up from Hamilton and brought a trailer with mattresses and tents and stuff, her husband's Kevin and their kids are Alex (18), Noah (14), and Paul (13), plus there's Grandma, Grandpa, and all of us. The big boys are sleeping in tents on the lawn, the adults are in the bedrooms, and Ethan and Tavita are on a mattress in Mum and Dad's room. They made a big fuss and said they should be allowed to sleep in the tents with the other boys. Dad told them to cut it out, but Mum said if they behave, we'll see.

Suz loved my boots. It made me feel great and made it worth it wearing them for the whole trip. By the time we had some dinner and talked and talked it was late, so

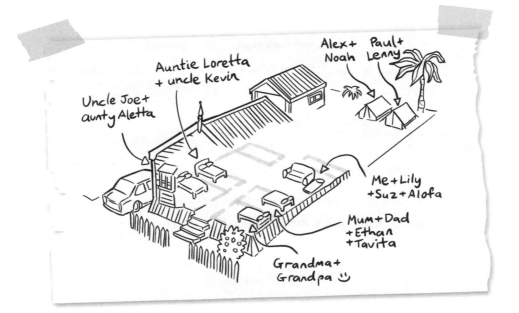

we got the mattresses out and made up our beds, then we got into bed and talked some more. I fell asleep listening to the adults talking Samoan. It sounds like a lot of vowel sounds all strung together.

TUESDAY, 12 October

Auntie Aletta cooked up plates and plates of toast for us kids, we must have eaten 4 loaves of bread. Then we heard that there's going to be a feast here on Saturday night for Lenny's 18th birthday. We have loads of relatives here in Auckland who want to come see us, so Dad, Uncle Joe, and the others decided to combine it with Lenny's 18th. Grandma and Grandpa have brought some palusami and taro from Samoa, so we'll be having that and there'll be a pig on a spit.

Grandma and Grandpa brought us presents. Lily and I got a turtle-shell bangle and shell beads. Dad and Lenny got a lavalava and a shirt, Ethan got a small log drum (which is pretty annoying right now), Tavita got a log canoe, and Mum got a fan, a jar of coconut oil, and some shell earrings. I guess she'll have to get her ears pierced now.

WEDNESDAY, 13 October

Lily, Ethan, Tavita, Suz, Alofa, Noah, Paul, and me went to the park this afternoon. The big boys had gone with Uncle Joe and Uncle Kevin to get tables and chairs and stuff for the feast. While we were at the park these kids from Suz's school came along and were calling us names, they said we were a bunch of afakasi with some swearwords as well. Noah and Paul wanted to fight them and I wanted to as well, I thought I could use my fancy cat-fighting skills on them hahaha.

I thought there really was going to be a fight when we heard Tavita yelling like Tarzan. At first I thought he was just trying to get in on the fight, but then we realised he had slipped from the rope-climbing thingy. He fell from quite high up and cracked his head on the concrete and a huge bump came up straightaway. The boys from Suz's school yelled "HA HA" and took off. Noah started throwing stones at them.

We got Tavita up and took him straight home. He screamed all the way—Mum said it sounded like a siren coming up the street. When Auntie Loretta saw it she started pushing the lump hard. Tavita screamed more and Mum looked really panicked. Auntie Loretta said this is what they do in the Islands. Mum decided to take Tavita to the hospital, so now Tavita has a patient card at Auckland Hospital as well.

They never got back until late. The doctors said to keep him quiet and rested for a couple of days. Well, good luck with that! I told Dad what happened and asked him what "afakasi" means. He said it's the Samoan word for "half-caste," which means someone who is half Samoan and half pālagi.

"Well, that's what we are, so what's the big deal? Why were those boys being mean about it?"

Dad said sometimes people use it to put people down. It's like saying you're only <u>half</u> of this and <u>half</u> of that, so you're not as good as people who are <u>full</u> Samoan or <u>full</u> pālagi. Blimmin' heck, I wish I had given those mean boys the bash.

Auntie Loretta taught some of us to play a card game called Sweepy. It was fun—I won twice. Go, me! You have to do lots of adding and thinking. It's a neat game, we're going to play it again tomorrow.

THURSDAY, 14 October

Dad and Lenny took me to the Polynesian Panthers' headquarters today. I thought it would be like on *Get Smart* where you have to go through lots of doors and it would be dark with concrete walls and stuff. But nah. Tigi was there and some guys with Afros were with him. I told Lenny he should grow an Afro—he just laughed. One of the guys spoke Samoan to Dad. Charlotte's mum and some other ladies were there too. Charlotte's mum gave me a big hug and said, "Hi, Sofia, it's great to see you again," then she hugged Lenny and introduced herself to Dad. I felt really sad for her, now I know what happened to her husband.

The Panthers call each other brother or sister, it makes it feel like a real club when you hear them say Brother Tigi or Sister Melani. I like it.

I gave the present from Charlotte to her mum. When she opened it she was a bit tearful. It was a bottle of perfume, called Charlie. "Goodness, how could Charlotte afford this?" I told her about the milk run. "Charlie—it will remind me of her every time I use it. Please tell

Charlotte I love it," she said. And then, "Actually, I'll write her a note," which she did there and then and sprayed some of the perfume on it. She gave me a squirt too. It smelled really pretty. The only thing we usually smell is Dad's Old Spice aftershave.

Dad made a bit of a speech to the Panthers to thank them for all their help getting Lenny off the arrest. Lenny said a few words too. Then Tigi told them it's important we stand together to fight injustice. Tigi gave Dad a legal aid booklet that the Panthers have made and Dad invited them to Lenny's birthday celebrations. I hope they come and bring the baby. There was a lot of talk about how the city council are talking about evicting the Panther Party from their premises so they can put a car park there. The Panthers aren't going to let that happen without a fight.

On the way back to Uncle Joe's, I said, "Tigi sounds like a real-life Martin Luther King Jr." Dad and Lenny agreed.

Maybe that's what my speech can be about . . . I'll do a mind map tomorrow.

FRIDAY, 15 October

Happy birthday to you, happy birthday to you, happy birthday, dear Lenny, happy birthday to you!

Yep, Lenny is 18 today. He got a tank top and two LPs from Mum and Dad, one is Bob Marley and the Wailers, the other is *20 Solid Gold Hits, volume 14.* Me and Lily got him a leather wallet and some chocolate peanuts. There's been tons of action here today—people making food, putting up tables, and setting out chairs.

Lenny went away with the men early this morning. There was massive excitement when they arrived back with a dead pig on the trailer. When they unloaded it, Lenny came inside and had a shower. We asked where the pig came from and he said he killed it with his own hands. We just laughed—but it turns out he did!

Us big kids squeezed into the boys' tent after tea and he told us about it. Dad told him they were going to get a pig for the spit, and Lenny thought they were just picking it up from the butcher's or something but when they got to the place, the pig was running around in a pen. Dad said, "This is the pig for your celebration, son. You need to kill it."

Lenny had been gobsmacked. He'd asked where the knife was and how he was supposed to do it. The men there all laughed, then the guy who owned the pig said, "You don't use a knife—you use a pole to kill it." The guy explained, "First you have to catch the pig, then use the pole to suffocate it."

"Ew ew ew," I said, covering my ears and running out of the tent. When they'd finished telling the story, they called me back in. I don't think it can have been very good because some of the kids were looking a bit pale.

Poor Lenny—there's no way I'm touching that pig, I won't be eating a bite. Lenny said all the men had patted him on the back and congratulated him. It was obviously some kind of a rite of passage for Island men.

EWW!! but

SUNDAY, 17 October

Wow, the party was fantast-a-mundo! We got to stay up until 1 o'clock in the morning. There's lots of cleaning up going on now, so I'm in the boys' tent hiding for a bit.

When we were getting ready for the party I asked Suz what she was wearing, and she had a really neat skirt and top, but she only had her school shoes to wear with it so I offered her my boots. I couldn't believe it when the words came out of my mouth, and as soon as I said it I was hoping she would say no. Of course she didn't.

"Seriously, Sofia? Oh man, that's so nice of you. But what will you wear?"

"Oh, I have my sandals," I said weakly.

"Okay—wow, thanks."

I don't know why I offered and I felt really sad about it at the start, but after a while I thought it was good seeing how great they looked on her.

We met heaps of relatives at the party and got kissed and hugged by a lot of people. Tigi and 2 of his friends, Aliu (who we met at the HQ) and Jimmy (who is Māori) came. They'd brought guitars, so they played some songs. I heard Lenny and Alex talking to them. They were saying things like, "Cool sounds, man," and, "I really dig it."

There was a bit of Island dancing, and us girls had to get up and do it too, but we weren't very good at it. Even my pālagi Mum had a go. I think she was better than us.

When it came time for the feast the men brought the whole pig in. It smelled amazing and when they cut it up and put it on the plates, I thought, Well it doesn't look like a pig now . . . so I ate some. It was so beautiful I had seconds. So much for not touching the pig! The food was so nice—I tried to have a bit of everything, even the taro, which I don't really like. I loved the palusami though, which is a very yummy taro leaf baked with coconut cream. We were only allowed a little bit of that so there would be plenty for the adults. Then there was pineapple pie for dessert—YUM!

The best part of the party was when Grandma and Grandpa got up to do some Island dancing. Their dancing was so gentle and beautiful, I want to learn to dance just like them.

MONDAY, 18 October

THIS IS THE WORST DAY OF MY LIFE!

Dad, Uncle Joe, Uncle Kevin, Lenny, and Alex have all been taken away by the police! They're at the jail. We are all just sitting around crying waiting to see what happens.

It all started about 4 o'clock this morning.

Everyone was sound asleep when we were woken by all this banging and shouting and a dog barking. Next thing we know, the lights are on and there are police standing in the lounge! Us girls start screaming and then everything goes MENTAL!

Some of the adults came running to see what's going on and the police start shouting at them to stop and back off. The police dog is growling and barking at Dad and Uncle Kevin. Then we hear screaming from one of the rooms—there's a policeman in there trying to pull Grandma and Grandpa out of bed!!! Grandma is hitting him with her jandal.

Dad runs up the hall and yells at the policeman to leave them alone. The policeman shouts at Dad to get back to the lounge and raises his baton. They make Dad stand in the corner and Grandma and Grandpa are told to sit on the couch. Us girls have to sit on the floor. We try to go and grab some blankets coz we're in our pj's but the policeman drags us back. Dad yells at him to get his hands off us and rushes over. Next thing, two cops have Dad with his arm bent up behind his back and they're putting him in the paddy wagon.

So much noise! So much confusion. None of us knows what's going on.

One policeman yells to another, "Geez, they're everywhere! The neighbour was right," and he pulls Ethan, Tavita, and Mum into the lounge too. "What's a nice white girl like you doing in a place like this?" he says to Mum.

Then we hear another cop swearing at Auntie Loretta and telling her to hurry up.

That's when Uncle Kevin loses his temper and rushes up the hallway. The police dog goes crazy, barking and snarling. Ethan is so scared that he wets his pants, and the policeman yells at Mum, "Oh for God's sake! Get this kid out of here, woman!"

That's the moment when Lenny and the boys get involved. Lenny goes berserk and hits the cop—bam!—in the face. The police dog grabs Lenny's arm and drags him to the floor.

So Lenny and Uncle Kevin end up in the paddy wagon too.

Tavita is hugging me and crying. "Are they going to shoot us, Sofia?"

I whisper back, "No, it'll be okay, just shush," then the policeman yells at me to shut up.

Once we're all sitting in the lounge, the policeman puts the dog outside. Then they start asking us who we are and demanding our identification papers. They start with Grandma and Grandpa, but they hardly speak any English so Uncle Joe tries to translate for them. The policeman tells him to shut up, but then, when he can't understand Grandma and Grandpa, he has to talk with Uncle Joe. Uncle Joe explains Grandma and Grandpa are visiting from Samoa and the cop lets him get their passports. Then Uncle Joe says that he, Dad, and Auntie Loretta have been in NZ for about 20 years and they all have NZ citizenship.

The policeman doesn't ask anything about Mum or Auntie Aletta. Probably because they're not Islanders. He did ask for the names of all us kids. Uncle Joe goes around naming everyone, but when he gets to Paul he says, "This is Baul." Because of his Island accent, his "p" sounds like a "b." The cop says, "Ball, what kind of a stupid name is that for a kid?"

I could see what was happening, so I tell the policeman it's Paul and he says, "I told you to shut the (F word) up."

Well—that's when Alex got put in the paddy wagon— and poor Uncle Joe too, coz he was trying to stop Alex from hitting the policeman, but the police all thought they were being attacked. So that's how all the men got taken to jail.

Grandma and Grandpa were crying and so were we. Now Mum and Auntie Aletta have gone to the Panthers' HQ to get some help.

3:00 p.m.

Everyone is back home now. Tigi and some Panther brothers are here talking with the adults. Lenny has a bandage on his arm from the dog bite—or should I say, the vicious dog attack!

TUESDAY, 19 October

The men told us all about what happened. On the way to jail, Lenny was shouting at the police asking what grounds they had for invading our privacy, asking for their badge numbers and stuff like that. He learnt about that from the legal aid booklet. It didn't help though, coz they wouldn't listen to him. Lenny said they were taken to jail and all put in separate cells. By lunchtime the Panthers were at the jail along with a guy called Hone Harawira, who's a member of Ngā Tamatoa (they're a Māori group, sort of like the Panthers I think), and David Lange (the lawyer guy). Lenny said Mr. Lange really is "da man." He did his lawyer talking and got them all released. He told the police the raid was illegal and that there will be action from the Panthers in response.

Afterwards, the Panthers and Hone came to Uncle Joe's to talk with the family. They gave out legal aid booklets and told Uncle Joe to spread the word to his friends about their rights. The Panthers and Ngā Tamatoa brought us food as well. I guess they knew everyone would be too upset to think about cooking, so that was really nice and helpful.

We think Uncle Joe's neighbour dobbed us in to the police because there were so many of us staying in the one house. He never bothered to find out why we were all there. Uncle Joe said the neighbor has never been very friendly and it didn't surprise him.

It's funny (not haha funny, just odd) how us kids all remember different things about what happened. Sometimes we found ourselves arguing about how it happened and in what order things happened—AS IF IT MATTERED!

WEDNESDAY, 20 October

Tavita has been glued to Dad since the raid. He even slept in Mum and Dad's bed last night. We had a quiet day. I think everyone is still upset. Grandma carries her hanky in her hand and keeps dabbing her eyes. Poor Grandma and Grandpa, this is not what their holiday should be like.

In the afternoon, all us kids—even Lenny and Alex—watched cartoons. The mums made us doughnuts, all crunchy and covered in icing sugar. When we'd finished, the boys licked the plates. We were watching *The Jetsons*, a cartoon about a space-age family. The mum was talking to her friend on a TV phone where they could see each other. It was early in the morning and Jane looked awful, but when the phone rang she had this mask of herself that she put on so her friend wouldn't see her without makeup. Then when Jane sneezed, the mask flew off! Haha.

Imagine . . . TV phones, where you can see the person you're talking to! Nah, can't ever see that happening, but Alex (who's science crazy), reckons it could. I think he's dreaming, there's no way! When the ads came on we had a competition to see who could sing the most words, me and Suz won with the Bernina ad: "Bernina, Bernina, so easy, simple, and versatile, Bernina, Bernina, gets all your sewing done in style, Bernina, Bernina, the experts all agree . . ." It's too long to write it all.

THURSDAY, 21 October

The grown-ups decided we needed to do something different today so we all went out to the shops. They have great sales in Auckland. I got some flared Wrangler jeans—yippeee! Dad bought this Polaroid camera. It cost $28 and he thought Mum would be angry at the cost but she wasn't at all. She just said, "It's a good idea to take photos of everyone when we're all together."

The camera is incredible. You take the photo and it automatically prints out of a slot in the bottom of the camera. It comes out sort of wet, then you just wait about 3 minutes for the picture to develop and dry. We wanted Dad to take a photo of us but he said it was for

group photos, although he did take 2 of Grandma and Grandpa on their own and gave one to them.

The best part of the day was getting buckets of Kentucky Fried Chicken for tea. Me and Suz sang the whole ad and everyone laughed. I don't think Grandma and Grandpa understood it but they thought it was funny too, probably because us kids were bobbing up and down like the kids in the back of the car on the cartoon ad do. "Hugo said you go, and I said no you go . . ."

Today was so much fun. I don't want to go home. We leave on Saturday . . . BOOOOOOHOOOOO . . .

FRIDAY, 22 October

Tigi and some of the Panthers came to see us today. Charlotte's mum too. She gave me a present for Charlotte, so I put it with the note she'd already given me. Tigi told us the police aren't pressing any charges against Dad and the others. In fact, he said we might have grounds for a case against them because of "police brutality," but Dad and the uncles said they didn't want to do that.

I had no idea people could press charges against the police. They're the police—they do the charging! I think Dad and the others should press charges. It's not fair that we were treated so badly, especially Grandma and Grandpa. I think they just don't want to rock the boat and get on the wrong side of the police.

When Suz and I went to the dairy to get bread, she was saying that her dad was going to make them go to school while we were staying here, but her mum said that wasn't fair. I'm glad they got to stay home. It wouldn't have been the same without her and Alofa around.

I told her about this dream I had last night where I was flying, and she said she has that dream too some-times. We talked about what happens in our flying dreams and how much we love it. Suz said she asked her family if they have that dream but none of them do. When we got back, I asked Lily if she does and she said no too, so me and Suz decided it's our own special thing. When I talked about having to avoid the power lines, Suz knew exactly what that was like. She talked about how, when she's trying to take off, she runs along and then jumps—and that's exactly what happens in my fly-ing dream. It was crazy that we both have the same dreams. We promised to write to each other all the time and we made a secret club, called SS, but I can't write what it stands for because we swore we would keep it our secret.

I can't believe the holiday is almost over.

SUNDAY, 24 October

We got home at 8 o'clock last night and had spaghetti on toast for tea. I had to make the toast but it took ages cooking it on the rack on the stove, then Lenny said to cook it in the oven. That was so much quicker. I could cook heaps at a time, and the toast was golden and super crunchy, I never thought toast could taste so good.

Leaving Auckland was horrible. Not as bad as being dawn-raided, but nearly.

No one wanted to start the goodbyes, and once they started, no one wanted to end them. It was so sad to see Dad saying goodbye to Grandma and Grandpa, they hugged and cried for ages, then I saw Dad put a roll of $5 notes into Grandpa's hand. Grandpa pretended to donk Dad on the head, then he patted him on the back.

Grandma said some things in Samoan to Mum. Dad told us later she was saying Mum was a good girl. (That's nice but she's not a girl, she's a lady.)

I kind of wanted to give my boots to Suz, but I just couldn't, so instead I gave her my halter-neck top. I put a note with it that said "SS Forever" with loads of hearts and kisses, and I drew a picture of me and her flying (teehee, I bet she likes that). I left it on her mattress to find after we'd gone.

On the trip home, no one knew what to say to Dad, so we were quiet and sad most of the way. We tried to play "I spy with my little eye," but you could tell no one was in the mood so that soon stopped.

When we finally got home, the animals were pleased to see us. Dad let Maile sleep in the boys' room and in the morning Mum said both boys and the dog were all in the same bed. She thinks the dawn raid has spooked the boys.

Rawiri ended up staying the night too, and sleeping on Lenny's floor. They talked about what happened in Auckland and I heard Rawiri swearing. Mum and Dad must have heard too coz Dad yelled out to them to tone it down. When Rawiri left, I gave him the present to take home for Charlotte.

There was so much washing and unpacking to do today I wanted a tent to run away and hide in, but Mum said if we all get stuck in, it will be easier. I'm glad there was no milk run today.

The Sunday Disney movie was *The Swiss Family Robinson*. We all loved it, but it made me miss everyone in Auckland. I couldn't believe it when Ethan said, "Look at Sofia, she's crying." I started blinking like crazy, but it didn't help.

Mum said, "We're all just tired out. Let's make it an early night."

Back to school tomorrow ... OH NO! I haven't worked on my speech at all!

MONDAY, 25 October

The milk run was hard today. Mum was right—I am tired out.

Charlotte loved the stuff from her mum. She said she could smell the perfume on her letter and the present was a love-bead bracelet, which she was wearing under her school jersey so it wouldn't get taken off her.

We talked at morning tea and lunchtime. She wanted to know everything about the dawn raid and about us visiting the Panthers HQ. I felt bad for Charlotte that I got to see her mum and she didn't.

TUESDAY, 26 October

I was meant to go to speech coaching with Mr. Carter today, but I couldn't tell him I hadn't done anything so I hid in the toilets for the whole lunchtime. I should've taken a book or something, coz it was a long time to wait, but it's interesting what happens in there at lunchtime.

Some girls were smoking, and then I heard a girl crying, and then I heard some girls talking about boys, and then there's me—hiding out. Wow! It's all go in the loos. I should hide there again and write a book about what happens. It might be a best seller. Or it might be a flop and go down the toilet ... hahahahaha, that's funny.

I got paid today for the week before we went away— what a nice surprise. I wasn't expecting to be paid.

WEDNESDAY, 27 October

Mr. Parker was back today, Charlotte said he hadn't been coming to school because he was down south visiting family—his wife (ex-wife) and daughter are in Dunedin. Huh, I didn't even know he was married. We did our old songs and then he taught us a new song. It's a poi song and we're going to make some poi and learn how to use them. Mr Parker showed us his set. Both are the same size. The ball and the attached plaited rope handles are red, black, and white, which he told us was because these are traditional colours used in Māori art. He also said using poi in song and dance takes a lot of skill and we need to practice heaps. There is so much to know about making poi. First we learned some tikanga, or rules, such as don't hit people with your poi. We also learned that traditionally poi were used by males and females to help strengthen wrists for war. I love it, we always do such fun stuff with him. I wonder if our rakau group will enjoy poi as much as rakau.

SATURDAY, 30 October

There was lots of mail today. Mum and Dad said they were mostly bills, so we all need to think about tightening our belts. I think it's a grown-ups way of saying we need to stop spending so much money. They said our holiday cost a lot more than they thought it would.

I asked if we should do a bottle drive to raise some money, but they laughed and said it's not that bad yet. Mum said we're going to plan out our meals for the week so the groceries will cost less. Me, Lenny, and Lily decided we can buy tea one night and split the cost between us. Mum and Dad said we don't need to do that, but Lenny said, "We're a team, remember," so they agreed. It really feels like we are a team. I think the dawn raid sort of pulled us closer together.

I was excited because there was a letter from Suz. She was ~~wrapped rapt~~ wrapt (don't know how to spell that) with the top and the note I left her. She signed her letter "SS Forever" as well and drew us flying on a bird, that was a cool idea.

She said Uncle Joe has been hanging out with Tigi and the Panthers and he is helping out however he can. When I told Dad and Lenny, they were pleased.

SUNDAY, 31 October

I worked on my speech today, but it didn't go very well. Still, at least I'll have something to show Mr. Carter this week.

MONDAY, 1 November

"A pinch and a punch for the first of the month."

TUESDAY, 2 November

There was no hiding from Mr. Carter. Right before lunch he came to the class to check I would be there. We all had to share where we were at with our speeches. The other 2 kids have done so much I felt embarrassed sharing what I had. Mr. Carter was great as usual though, and he said some nice things about all our speeches and then gave us some tips. He told me that my topic was spot-on and said if I can find a way to hook people into it, I would be on track. Next week is the last meeting before the competition so we are going to read our speeches to each other. I might have to take a week off school to prepare!

WEDNESDAY, 3 November

After the milk run tonight, us kids shouted fish 'n' chips for dinner. I got one piece of fish and made some hot chip sandwiches as well. It was good helping out, and we're going to do it again next Wednesday.

Yay, it was Mr. Parker day at school. We made our poi and learnt to do a four-plait rope for the handle. We used this fabric stuffing for the inside of the poi. It's like the stuffing you can see on the arm of our couch where the material has worn through. We cut up plastic rubbish bags to make the outsides of the balls. It was hard to get them all the same size. We all laughed at Jonathan's coz they were about the size of a small soccer ball!

"You might break your wrists if you try to use those," Mr. Parker said, so Jonathan had to pull them apart and start again. Next week we're going to learn how to use poi and the actions for the waiata. EXCITING!

FRIDAY, 5 November

Guy Fawkes' Day! There's going to be a bonfire at the boys' primary tonight.

SATURDAY, 6 November

Last night we all went to the bonfire at the boys' school. Charlotte and Rawiri came too, and Jonathan was there with his family. Dad knew Jonathan's dad coz they're from the same village in Samoa. The fireworks display was cool, except it was a bit scary when one big firework fell over and shot into the trees. The men spent ages pouring buckets of water over the area to make sure it didn't start a fire.

Us kids had some sparklers and Tom Thumb crackers. Jonathan hung out with me and Charlotte and when it was time to go, his father spoke to him in Samoan—and Jonathan answered in Samoan. I'm so jealous, I wish I could speak Samoan, then I'd be able to talk to Grandma and Grandpa. I don't know why Dad's never taught us. Probably because Mum doesn't speak it, so English is what we've always spoken at home. Maybe Jonathan could teach me. When they were leaving, Jonathan's dad said, "OI, boy, go get your goat."

I said, "What? Why would you bring a goat to a bonfire?" Jonathan laughed and laughed and laughed. It turns out his dad was saying "coat" but his "g" sounds like a "c" because of his Samoan accent. I was thinking, Geez, are they going to kill the goat like Lenny had to kill the pig? But no, thank goodness, it's just a coat.

SUNDAY, 7 November

You won't believe this! NOW Ethan has a BROKEN ARM!!!

He and Archie were sliding down the banister at Archie's house (which they are NOT s'posed to do). Ethan slipped and fell to the floor below—right from the top, and it's really high. No one knew for sure if his arm was broken, but Mum made Dad take him to the hospital this time. She said she was sick of showing her face there.

Lenny went with Dad and they were gone for ages. When they got back, Ethan's arm was in a plaster cast. I tried to make a joke: "Hey, Ethan's a half-caste in a cast." It wasn't a good time for a joke apparently. Poor Ethan, it must hurt because he wasn't really crying, he was just sort of whimpering—a lot. Mum had to give him some

Disprin, which made him whimper even more. Dad said the doctors were great and one of them even signed Ethan's cast and told him to try and get the whole thing covered in signatures before he comes back to get it off in 6 weeks.

WOW! 6 weeks with a cast on. Ethan is the first person to have a broken bone in our family. He has to have a few days off school. Lucky him.

MONDAY, 8 November

Charlotte's mum is back for a surprise visit and is staying until Christmas. After that she may be away for a long time because there's going to be some big protest thing going on with the people from Charlotte's tribe. Her iwi is called Ngāti Whātua. The protest is something to do with Māori land and stuff, and the Panthers and Ngā Tamatoa and heaps of other human rights groups might get involved. It's going to start in January, but they have no idea how long it will go for.

I wonder if Dame Whina Cooper is leading this one. Maybe Uncle Joe will be involved, since he's been hanging out with the Panthers. Oh, I found out his real name is Iosefa—that's much better than Joe.

TUESDAY, 9 November

I got to stay home today to look after Ethan, coz Mum and Dad had a meeting at the bank in Wellington and then had some jobs to do. I made us pancakes with syrup for lunch and had to cut Ethan's up for him. They were yum—all crispy around the edges. Dad taught me to make them. He said butter is what makes them good, so I used lots. We played some Chinese checkers and draughts, then Ethan fell asleep for a while. Mum and Dad got home after 3 o'clock, so they picked Tavita up from school on the way and bought some lamingtons with cream for afternoon tea. I had 2, they were yum.

At about 4 o'clock there was a knock at the door, which freaked the boys out. I told them it was okay because I could hear Dad talking to whoever it was. I wandered out to see who it was and was shocked to see Mr. Carter. He had a note for me with the details about the speech competition. Dad invited him in and Mum made a cup of tea. Lucky we hadn't eaten all the lamingtons. I think he thought Mum had made them and he was pretty impressed.

He asked how my speech was going—I had forgotten we were supposed to be sharing today! I said I was still working on it, so he asked if he could hear what I had. I told him it was at school in my desk so he said he would check in with me during the week.

I looked at the details for the competition that he'd brought around. My age group starts at 11:00 a.m. and we have to be there 20 minutes beforehand. There are 6 kids in my age group from different colleges—and I'm first! Then there's a half-hour break for the judges to discuss after each section before placings are announced. I feel really nervous now!

WEDNESDAY, 10 November

Poi day was really neat! Some of the moves were easy, but some were hard. I brought mine home to practise. FUN FUN FUN. I can see this is going to be the new lunchtime thing to do.

At the end of the day Mr. Morrison told the class about my speech competition this weekend. Argh, no! I didn't want everyone to know. Mr. Parker asked if he could come along to support me. He said he would come with Charlotte, Rawiri, and Charlotte's mum.

"WHAT? I didn't expect people to come and listen."

Mr. Parker said, "It's about people wanting to support you, girl." I hadn't thought about that. I liked that Mr. Parker called me "girl" like he does with Charlotte. Maybe I'll get to call him Uncle Piripi one day too.

Fish 'n' chips night again. I had a battered hot dog and sauce tonight.

THURSDAY, 11 November

I worked on my speech for ages last night, until Mum came and told me I needed to turn the light off and go to sleep. I didn't want to stop, especially now I know people are coming to listen! I got my torch out and tried to work on it under the blankets, but that was too hard, so I pulled one corner of my bedspread across to the chest of drawers and tucked it into the top drawer, which made a sort of tent. It worked really well and I wrote until I could hardly see. I was pretty tired at school today, but it was worth it. Mr. Carter was pleased with it. He had some ideas about a few changes I could make.

FRIDAY, 12 November

Mr. Arbuckle came into class to wish me well for the speech competition, Mum said that was nice.

Katrina was away today so Charlotte was doing the milk run. She asked me about my speech then asked what I was going to wear. I hadn't even thought about that. I said my boots for sure, but I didn't have a good skirt

to go with them, then Charlotte said she has a green suede skirt and matching battle jacket that I could borrow and they would look great with the boots.

Rawiri brought Charlotte over after tea. The skirt and battle jacket are SO FUNKY! I tried them on with my boots and showed everyone, they said it looked FAB. Lily is going to do a hair plait for me too, so even if my speech doesn't go well, at least I'll look good.

SUNDAY, 14 November

Yesterday was da bomb!

I got up early and practised my speech in the bathroom so I could see myself in the mirror to check I was making eye contact with the audience. I timed myself again too. I didn't eat breakfast. Mum kept trying to make me, but I just couldn't.

When we got to the competitions the 11 to 12 age group were just finishing, so we waited for the break, then went in and took a seat. The judges came onstage to announce that a girl from Titahi Bay Intermediate won that section.

I looked around and saw Charlotte and her mum sitting with Rawiri and Mr. Parker. Behind them were Mr. Carter and Mr. Morrison with Tania, Colin, Walter, and Jonathan. Oh, crumbs! I didn't know if it was good or bad having them all there. Mr. Carter came over and said, "Sofia, your speech is fantastic and you have an important message to get across, so try to enjoy yourself."

Huh, there was nothing enjoyable about this! I was starting to fidget so I sat on my hands to keep them still—they were feeling sweaty.

The announcer introduced the next age group and the judges, who were a Radio Windy host, an *Evening Post* reporter, and a lady who has some big business whose name I can't remember.

Next thing, I heard my name called and I got a ringing sound in my ears as I got up and walked onto the stage. The hall was about half full and I stared at the crowd. The announcer said, "Welcome, Sofia. Your time starts now!"

I smiled (like Mr. Carter told us to), breathed in (like he said to), and opened my mouth (I thought of that bit myself, haha). Then I said:

"*Talofa lava and good morning. I am Sofia Christina Savea. My speech is called 'Polynesian Panthers—Gang Members or Good Guys?'*

"*Imagine this: You're having an amazing family holiday, one where everyone is there and all 18 of you are squeezed into one house. Kids are playing outside, adults are talking inside, there's food and games and laughing. The teenagers are sleeping out the back in a tent, the younger kids are on mattresses on the floor, the adults are sleeping in the bedrooms, and it's the **best** family holiday ever.*

"*Fast forward to 4 o'clock in the morning, and there's banging and yelling and screaming. The police are in the house, pulling people out of bed. They have a dog with them—it's snarling and barking, kids are crying and everyone is confused. Mums are crying and hugging kids, grandparents are scared. Some of the men are taken away in a paddy wagon.*

"*It sounds like a made-up horror story, doesn't it? But it's not. It's real. It's called a dawn raid, and it's something that has been happening to Pacific Island people for the past 2 years. How do I know this? Because it happened to me and my family last month when we were on holiday in Auckland.*"

I paused for a moment here. The judges' eyes were wide and they sat up a bit in their seats.

"It was terrifying—and it should never have happened. You probably have lots of questions about why the police would do something like this to a family who are enjoying a fun holiday together and have done nothing wrong. It's all to do with the current economic crisis and the government cracking down on overstayers. Now, you might be thinking, Okay, so what's an overstayer? That's someone who has asked to come to Aotearoa/New Zealand to work or visit, but then has not returned to where they came from when their work or visitor permits ran out. So they become 'overstayers.' There are a lot of overstayers in New Zealand, from countries all over the world, but the government has

targeted ONLY Pacific Islanders, who make up just thirty-three percent of the overstayers. The other sixty-six percent are from European countries. However, the government has been carrying out dawn raids on Polynesians for a long time.

Two of the judges whispered to each other, which put me off a bit. I didn't know if it was because they liked my speech or they didn't like it.

"By now you may be thinking, What happened to the people who were taken away in the paddy wagons? They were taken to the police station and locked in cells. There was no time to get dressed so some were in their lavalavas and some had bare feet. They were frightened, confused, and angry.

"The people who were left at home didn't know what to do, so they contacted some friends who are members of a group called the Polynesian Panthers. The Panthers came to help them. They got them out of jail, taught them about their rights, and even brought them food after the raid.

"In news reports, the Polynesian Panthers have been talked about as troublemakers—gang members who are hostile and militant, which means sort of army-like. If you visit the Panthers headquarters in Auckland—and yes, having a headquarters sounds like something from Get Smart *but it's not like that"*—the people all laughed when I said that—*"what you will find is a group that is focused, organised, caring, strong, and brave. Yes, it is true that the Panthers have had to stand up for what they believe is right, and it is because of them the public is learning about the dawn raids.*

"Here is some of the good work they're doing." I held the booklet up here. "*They have created a legal aid booklet that tells people what to do to protect themselves if they are picked on unfairly. They have started homework clubs to help kids succeed at school. They help the elderly people in their community by doing gardening and odd jobs . . . and they challenge the government on behalf of Pacific Island people. I wonder how much of that has been reported in the news.*

"Let me tell you more about the Panthers. They have branches throughout New Zealand, even as far away as Dunedin. They have been here in Porirua recently, teaching people about their rights, and they marched with the hīkoi in October last year. A Polynesian Panther called Brother Tigilau Ness brought a group here and told people about a man called Che Guevara, who inspired him so much that Tigilau named his son after him. Ernesto Che Guevara, or 'Che,' was an Argentinian leader and revolutionary who believed* *in standing up for the rights of others. In his words, 'Above all, always be capable of feeling deeply any injustice committed against anyone, anywhere in the world.'*

"My family was lucky to have the Polynesian Panthers to support us when we were dawn-raided and treated unfairly. The Panthers told us, adults and children, that we are now part of the change that needs to happen. They also told us that Che Guevara believed that the first duty of a revolutionary is to be educated.

"If you had asked me 2 months ago if I could make a difference in the world, I would have said, 'I'm only 13, what can I do to make a difference?' But now I see that anyone can make a difference, like Tigilau taught us. We can 'educate to liberate,' which means we need to get informed about what is going on around us and teach others. Whether you're a child or an adult, you can make a change—find out, get information, share it with others. Information is power!

"What I have learned is, what we hear in the news depends on who is doing the reporting. So is everyone getting a fair point of view about what's really happening?

"Maybe the title of my speech should change from 'Polynesian Panthers—Gang Members or Good Guys?' to 'News Media—Fair or Biased?'

"Fa'afetai lava—thank you."

I wasn't sure if I breathed at all during the speech but I let out a big breath when I finished. Everyone started clapping and I could hear my supporters whistling and shouting. As I went to step away from the microphone, Mr. Parker, Charlotte, her mum, Mr. Morrison, Mr. Carter, Tania, Colin, Walter, and Jonathan all stood up and sang "Tūtira Mai Ngā Iwi." I realised they were doing the song of support—a waiata tautoko—that Mr. Parker had told us about in class.

I froze, and then tears started rolling down my cheeks. I didn't have a hanky so I had to wipe my face on Charlotte's jacket. (Sorry, Charlotte!) When they finished, people clapped for them as well—it was very cool.

I sat down beside Dad and he put his arm around my shoulder. I wouldn't normally want him to do that in public, but I was okay with it. I sat through the other speeches without even taking in what they were about. All I could think about was the waiata tautoko and how good it made me feel.

When it came time for judging, all 6 competitors had to stand on the stage and get feedback from the judges. I was first.

The business lady judge started, and she was cool. "Sofia, let me start by saying I admire your confident point of view and your hard-hitting message."

The radio guy was next. "Strong delivery, Sofia. Your pauses, timing, and audience engagement were superb."

The media guy said, "Wow, Sofia—you should consider a career in journalism yourself." I felt chuffed about that.

Then the business lady added, "By the way, love, your fashion sense is impeccable. I love your look!"

I looked at Charlotte, she smiled and gave me the thumbs-up.

I came 2nd. The winner's speech was called "The World of Fashion." I don't remember much about it, but Mum said it was very good. I got a book voucher and a bookmark for coming 2nd.

I had to do my milk run after that, which was a bit of a letdown, but when I got home I got a HUGE surprise. I walked in to a crowd singing, "For she's a jolly good fellow." I was thinking, Wha-a-a-at? It's not my birthday, then Dad came over and put his arm around my shoulder (again) and said, "Sofia Christina Savea, you're a winner in our eyes."

Oh! It was a celebration party for my speech. Flippin' heck!!!!! I started to cry again. Everyone who came to the speech competition was there, plus Charlotte's auntie, a few other cousins, and Archie, of course.

Mr. Parker brought his guitar so our group and Mr. Morrison did the songs he taught us. I wish we had our poi and rakau so we could've done that too. Then everybody sang heaps of songs, like "Ten Guitars" and "The Green Door." I was sitting on the floor beside Lily as she sang loudly. "What's those words you're singing?" I asked her.

"Gringo, what's that secret you're keeping . . ." she sang to me.

Everyone around us cracked up, and Lily said, "What?"

"It's 'green door' not 'gringo,'" Mum told her, laughing. Maybe it's a family thing that we don't know the proper words to songs. Anyway, we sang it some more—this time with Lily's words—so now the song is called "Gringo" in our family!

Everyone had brought food and Mum and Dad made a chop suey, cornbeef stew, and rice. We sang and talked and laughed for hours. The boys eventually fell asleep on the couch and Dad carried them to bed.

I think the best bit of the party was when Charlotte told me her favourite thing was the CORNBEEF stew. We've come a long way since that day we had the fight! It looks like our families are going to be great friends. How funny would it be if Charlotte and I end up best friends!!!

HISTORICAL NOTE

In 1976, things like colour television, bikes, family holidays, and Polaroid cameras were considered luxury items in New Zealand. This indicates that Sofia's family was in a comfortable financial position. Having two parents earning incomes would have contributed to this stability. The main takeaway food available at the time was fish and chips, which was still considered a special treat. Takeaway outlets had not long been on the scene in New Zealand; as Sofia explains, McDonald's had only just opened in 1976 in Porirua. Kentucky Fried Chicken (now called KFC) had opened five years earlier in Auckland, and Pizza Hut had opened just two years earlier, in 1974.

Sport was a popular pastime for children in the 1970s. Girls were beginning to take up sports once considered only for boys, such as cricket, soccer, and rugby. Boys were also being encouraged to play netball, but not many took it up. Television was one of the most popular pastimes for kids, and it had a start and a finish time, unlike now, where it runs for 24 hours a day. In 1980, the Goodnight Kiwi (a cartoon kiwi and his cat) would signal the end of broadcasting each day. He was retired in 1994, when 24-hour television transmission began.

Milk deliveries used to be in the early hours of the morning, so empty milk bottles would be put out at the gate at night with money or tokens left in the bottles. After around 1972, afternoon milk deliveries (like Sofia and Lenny's) replaced the early morning milk runs.

Music at the time was hugely influenced by the "disco" era—a breakaway from more traditional folk and country styles. Disco fashion for women included hot pants and platform shoes, and no makeup bag was complete without glitter

Milk runs were a common way for kids to earn pocket money.
Credit: Evening post, Alexander Turnbull Library, Ref: 1/4-022793-F.

gel, which was used in large quantities up the sides of the cheeks. Men's fashion included polyester suits with pointy collars on shirts or jackets and flared trousers. "Mullet" or "shaggy cut" hairstyles were all the go for men and women.

Gender roles were shifting. Traditionally, boys did woodwork and metalwork classes, and girls did home economics (cooking), sewing, and typing classes, but by the mid-1970s, all of these classes were offered to both genders.

Māori language and culture had only begun to feature in some schools at the time. This was largely due to Māori people asserting their rights to reclaim land, language, and identity. In 1973, Ngā Tamatoa (a Māori political group) presented a petition to the government to support Māori language in schools. The use of Māori language in schools had been suppressed, especially from the 1940s, with many elderly Māori people reporting how they had been punished for using te reo (the language of) Māori at school. Māori did not become an official language of New Zealand until 1987.

The 1970s were an era of protest, rights, and liberation, perhaps spurred on by prominent overseas rights advocates of the 1960s, such as Martin Luther King Jr.,

In the 1960s, thousands of people migrated from the Pacific Islands to fill labour shortages in the New Zealand workplace.
Credit: Auckland War Memorial Museum.

Malcolm X, and Rosa Parks from America, and Ernesto "Che" Guevara from Argentina leading the way and standing up for people's rights and justice. In New Zealand, women's rights were at the forefront, with groups demanding equal pay for equal work, and women wanting a say in issues that affected them. The Polynesian Panther movement in New Zealand was heavily influenced

Māori protesters form a mile-long march before arriving at Parliament, 1975. *Credit:* Alexander Turnbull Library, Ref: PA7-15-08.

by the American Black Panthers, with similarly held beliefs about fighting oppression and injustice. The Black Panther Party was formed in 1966 by co-founders Huey P. Newton and Bobby Seale with the purpose of challenging police brutality against Black citizens. The Black Panthers were easily recognised in their trademark black berets and leather jackets. Alongside their original purpose of monitoring police activity, their goals also included gaining positions for Black people in political office. They instigated change from within their own communities with breakfast clubs for children, which at their peak included 20,000 children across America—the Black Panther Party believed in the power of education and they wanted young people to turn up to school fed and ready to learn. They also initiated homework clubs, health care clinics, and many other social programs. The group officially ceased in 1982 due to a number of factors, including prolonged external pressure from the government and internal issues from within the group. Some original members remain active to this day as they continue to pass on knowledge of their experiences through public speaking engagements. Artist Emory Douglas, whose artwork featured in the Black Panther Party newspaper, continues to create murals and other graphic artworks with messages that highlight past and current injustices.

Gay rights were beginning to become more prominent in New Zealand, with groups more visible and vocal about their needs. During this decade people in the country were also protesting nuclear testing in the Pacific, the Vietnam War, and apartheid in South Africa.

Although Lenny, Sofia, and sometimes Lily were vocal about their points of view, challenging their parents in this way would rarely have occurred, especially in Pacific Island households, where respect for elders and service to the family were of high importance. Older children often cared for younger siblings, and children answering back to their parents would have been virtually unheard of. There were clear divisions between adulthood and childhood; you were either a child or an adult, and advancing to adulthood usually happened when you left school and joined the workforce or went to university.

Tigilau Ness is a real person and a Polynesian Panther. He did name his son Che after Ernesto "Che" Guevara, the Cuban revolutionary leader who was born in Argentina. Che (Tigilau's son), became known as Che Fu and built a successful hip-hop music career. Other prominent Panthers' children include musicians Scribe (son of Fa'amoana Luafutu, known as "John"), and Danny Leaosavaii (known as "Brotha D"—cofounder of the hip-hop music label Dawn Raid, named as an acknowledgment to this era in New Zealand history). Members of Leaosavaii's family had been targets of the dawn raids. Hip-hop artist King Kapisi (aka Bill Urale) publishes music under the name Overstayer and has a clothing

Polynesian Panther Party headquarters, Auckland.
Credit: Auckland Star.

A Polynesian Panthers demonstration.
Credit: John Miller.

label of the same name—also reminders of this period and the events of the time.

David Lange did become Prime Minister of New Zealand, representing the Labour Government from 1984 to 1989. He was a strong supporter and adviser for the Polynesian Panther group, especially from 1971 to 1976.

So, what happened to the people who were arrested in the dawn raids? They were taken away with only the clothes on their backs and were kept in cells until their paperwork could be produced. Those who *were* over-stayers were held until they were deported—some of them never saw their families again. It was a sad time that set friends and family members against each other, with some people dobbing others in to take the heat off themselves.

Random checks were carried out on the streets—a humiliating process. New Zealand–born–and–bred people were being stopped by police, simply because of the colour of their skin or the clothes they were wearing. Many police officers were opposed to "blitzing" Pacific Islanders with these random checks on the streets. A television news broadcast reported that they felt these

An after-school homework program organized by the Polynesian Panthers.
Credit: John Miller.

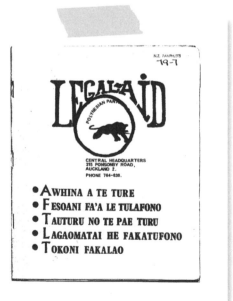

The Polynesian Panther Party *Legal Aid* booklet cover, 1973–1974.
Credit: Melani Anae.

A Christmas party organized by the Polynesian Panthers.
Credit: John Miller.

A Polynesian Panthers demonstration at the U.S. Consulate.
Credit: John Miller.

practises represented a step backwards in relations between police and Pacific people. There were many instances where television and newspapers did investigate and highlight injustices, probing politicians and police leaders to come clean about what was really happening.

The bulk of overstayers around this time—about two-thirds—were in fact from Australia, North America, and European countries. Pacific Island overstayers accounted for only one-third. However, Caucasians were not "dawn raided," and the largest number of people prosecuted for overstaying were Pacific Island people.

The Polynesian Panthers were a group of mainly New Zealand–born Pacific Islanders, aged from 17 to 20. Their number also included some Māori and Indian members. Unlike their parents and grandparents, who kept their heads down, never complained, and did all they could to fit in, the Panthers were prepared to address blatant injustices and stand up to authority. This often caused tension within families. To this day, Polynesian Panthers remain active in their communities, and some speak at schools and universities about their experiences and continue to pass on the important messages

Opening of the Dawn Raid exhibition, created by Pauline Vaeluaga Smith, 2019. From left to right: Tour manager Darren Vaeluaga, Polynesian Panthers Will'Ilolahia (Co-founder), Pauline Vaeluaga Smith (author of *Dawn Raid*, and newest and most Southern Polynesian Panther), and original Panther members Tigilau Ness, Dr Melani Anae, and Reverend Alec Toleafoa."

of "educate to liberate," "knowledge is power," and "power to the people." One of their strong beliefs is, "once a Panther, always a Panther."

Sofia's growing awareness of these issues could have ignited a career in law, education, or media. Or, knowing her fondness for fashion, perhaps she became a dancer for the popular *Ready to Roll* TV show and got a pair of go-go boots in every colour! Or, maybe both!

GLOSSARY

NEW ZEALAND
ENGLISH WORDS AND SLANG

Blew off – Broke wind or farted

Bottle drive – A popular way to fundraise in New Zealand prior to the 1980s. Beer and fizz bottles made of glass were collected by groups who went door to door. Bottles were returned to bottling plants, which gave refunds for these.

Brassed off – To be annoyed

Buzz – A maths game where a chosen number or multiple of this number is replaced with the word *buzz*. The first person starts counting from the number 1, progressing around the circle with each person saying the next number. If the number or multiple of this is said instead of *buzz* you would be eliminated from the game.

Cake cooler – A heavy wire rack used for putting baking aside to cool

Chooks – Chickens; in this story they are precooked chickens purchased from the supermarket

Chuffed – Really pleased with yourself

College – The New Zealand equivalent of junior high and high school

Dairy – A convenience store often located on a street corner

Dobbed in – To tell on another person

Element – The hotplate on a stovetop

Fizz – Fizzy soft drink or soda pop

Flash – Very fancy

Foofed – Extremely tired

Hard case – A funny or comical person

Hokey-pokey – A type of honeycomb toffee. New Zealand also has hokey-pokey ice cream, which is vanilla ice cream with solid chunks of hokey-pokey throughout.

Jandal – A thong or flip-flop

Jersey – A knitted cardigan or jumper

Lamingtons – Small squares of sponge cake coated all over with brown or pink icing and then coated with dried or desiccated coconut

Mutton bags – A stockinette-type meat bag used to keep meat clean. It has always been popular in New Zealand to repurpose these as cleaning cloths.

NAC – New Zealand National Airways Corporation

Nut roll bar – A candy bar filled with nuts and nougat and covered with chocolate

Overstayer – A person who has outstayed their permitted visit in a country

Pacific Islanders – People with Pacific Island heritage

Paddy wagon – A police van used for transporting people who have been arrested

Pikelet – A sweetened, round, small pancake or hotcake

Plait – A hair braid

Polynesian – A collective term used to describe people from Pacific Islands

Rusks – A hard biscuit usually for babies to chew on when they are teething

Scrummy – Super delicious

Shout dinner – To pay for dinner for others

Sooky la la – A sensitive person or a cry baby

Sultana – A dried grape like a raisin

Togs – Swimsuit

Top Town – A New Zealand game show series where teams from different towns competed against each other in various obstacle challenges

Torch – Flashlight

MĀORI WORDS

Aotearoa – The Māori name for New Zealand. The literal translation is Land of the Long White Cloud.

Hāngi – A traditional Māori method for cooking food in a pit oven in the ground

Hikoi – To walk or march. Indicating a long march or journey.

Iwi – A large group, tribe, or clan of people

Ka pai – Your work is good

Karakia – A prayer

Kumara – A sweet potato

Māori – Indigenous people of Aotearoa New Zealand

Marae – A gathering space with sacred buildings and grounds where special meetings are held

Pākehā – New Zealanders primarily of European descent. The term is also applied to fair-skinned people and has been extended to any non-Māori New Zealander.

Poi – Small, soft ball attached to a plaited rope. Poi are swung and used in dance performance.

Rakau – Sticks usually made of wood used in games as seen in the illustration on p. 45

Te Hapua – A town in the far north of New Zealand

GLOSSARY

Te reo Māori – The Māori language

Tikanga – Customs, rules, traditions

Waiata – Song

SAMOAN WORDS

Afakasi – Half caste. A person with European and Pacific Island ancestry.

Alofa – Love. Can also be a name.

Fa'afetai lava – Thank you

Lavalava – A sarong-type garment tied at the waist or hips

Pālagi – A non-Samoan person, usually fair-skinned

Palusami – A food made from taro leaves and coconut milk

Pasifika – A term used to describe migrants from the Pacific region and their descendants

Taro – A starchy root vegetable

Tapa – Coarse cloth made from the bark of the mulberry tree and decorated with Pacific designs

BIBLIOGRAPHY

BOOKS

Anae, M., L. Luli, & L. Burgoyne, eds. *Polynesian Panthers: The Crucible Years 1971–1974*. Auckland: Reed Publishing, 2006.

Anae, M., L. Luli, & L. Tamu, eds. *Polynesian Panthers: Pacific Protest and Affirmative Action in Aotearoa NZ 1971–1981*. Wellington: Huia Publishers, 2005.

Mallon, S., K. U. Mahina-Tuai, & D. I. Salesa, eds. *Tangata O Le Moana: New Zealand and the People of the Pacific*. Wellington: Te Papa Press, 2012.

Saisoa'a, M. 'Ngā hekenga hau. "Pacific Peoples in Aotearoa/New Zealand," in T. Ka'ai, J. Moorfield, M. Reilly, & S. Moseley, eds. *Ki te whaio: An Introduction to Māori Culture and Society*. Auckland: Pearson Education, 2004.

OTHER SOURCES

History.com Editors. (November 3, 2017). *Black Panthers*. Retrieved from https://www.history.com/topics/civil-rights-movement/black-panthers

King Collier, A. (November 4, 2015). *The Black Panthers: Revolutionaries, Free Breakfast Pioneers*. In National Geographic: Retrieved from https://

BIBLIOGRAPHY

www.nationalgeographic.com/culture/food/the-plate/2015/11/04/the
-black-panthers-revolutionaries-free-breakfast-pioneers/

McCartney, M. *Milk and Honey*. New Zealand: McCartney Productions,
2012. Documentary.

Ministry for Culture and Heritage. "Key Events 1976," in *The 1970s*.
Retrieved from https://nzhistory.govt.nz/culture/the-1970s/1976.

Ministry for Culture and Heritage. "McDonald's Arrives in New Zealand,"
in *The 1970s*. Retrieved from https://nzhistory.govt.nz/page/mcdonalds
-arrives-new-zealand.

NZ On Screen. *Dawn Raids*. Retrieved from https://www.nzonscreen.com
/title/dawn-raids- 2005.

Radio New Zealand. *Polynesian Panthers*. Retrieved from http://www
.radionz.co.nz/international/pacific-news/306630/how-the-polynesian
-panthers-gave-rise-to-pasifika-activism. Audio.

Spoonley, P. "Ethnic and Religious Intolerance: Intolerance Towards Pacific
Migrants," in *Te Ara: The Encyclopedia of New Zealand*. Retrieved from
http://www.TeAra.govt.nz/en/video/28181/a-raid-on-pacific-islanders.

ACKNOWLEDGMENTS

I acknowledge the courageous and adventurous Pacific pioneers who migrated to Aotearoa for a better life for themselves and their children. To the Polynesian Panthers and supporters who stood against injustice and empowered people to stand up for their rights, I am in awe of your determination, resilience, and bravery. I acknowledge the late Prime Minister, David Lange, who stood up for people when they needed his support. A massive fa'afetai to Alini Finlayson, Tigilau Ness, Johnny Penisula, Dr. Melani Anae, and Reverend Alec Toleafoa for sharing personal stories and experiences of the dawn raid era.

Much alofa to my friends and family who have walked this journey with me offering feedback and encouragement: the support crew, Junior Tonga, Tania Carran-Tonga, Ari Edgecombe, Gordy Ballantyne, Christina Jeffery, Colin Jeffery, Mary O'Rourke, Victor Rodger, Lyn

McDonald, and Mavis Penisula. Paula Woods, thank you for having your ears open and connecting the dots with Lynette Evans and Penny Scown, Scholastic NZ.

Warmest thanks to team Levine Querido, especially the wonderful Nick Thomas, it has been a joy working with you and the talented Mat Hunkin.

My heartfelt thanks to my number one proofreader and cheerleader Chris Horwell (the best SS ever), also number two, Mandy Smith, and number three, my Mum, who loves my work. I have to ask, do reviews count if they come from your Mum?

MY FAMILY, Geoff you win the "Oscar" for best male in a supporting role. Sarah and Mandy, I can hardly believe how lucky I am to have children who inspire me so. For my grandchildren Caden, Brooklyn, Indy, Ella, and Ali, you are the fuel for my soul.

ABOUT THE AUTHOR

Dawn Raid is the debut book by Pauline Vaeluaga Smith. For it, she received Best First Book at the New Zealand Book Awards for Children and Young Adults and a Storylines NZ Notable Book Award. Pauline's heritage is Samoan, Tuvaluan, Scottish, and Irish. Her work is heavily influenced by her experiences growing up in the 1970s, her roles as a teacher and university educator, her passion for civil rights and justice, and her deep interest in uplifting NZ Māori and Pasifika culture. She lives in a small seaside town at the bottom of the South Island of Aotearoa-New Zealand.

ABOUT THE ILLUSTRATOR

Mat Hunkin is an award-winning illustrator who has drawn for children's books, films, graphic novels, advertising, and magazines. Of Samoan and pālagi descent, Mat has a passion for illustrating history and sharing stories that matter with young readers. He currently works in the film industry in Auckland, New Zealand, enjoying the beach and bike rides with his wife and two children.

SOME NOTES ON THIS BOOK'S PRODUCTION

The art for the jacket and interiors was created by Mat Hunkin. Mat began his career as an illustrator using traditional pencil, ink, and wash techniques, and draws on those skills when working digitally. He enjoys the research process in illustration and design, especially sourcing reference images for historic details. The text was set by Westchester Publishing Services in Danbury, CT, in Adobe Jenson, a typeface drawn in 1996 by the company's chief designer, Robert Slimbach. A revival of Nicolas Jenson's roman and Ludovico Vicentino degli Arrighi's italic from the 15th and 16th centuries, Adobe Jenson is a serif noted for its elegance, readability, and flexibility as a typeface. The title type was set in Colby Compressed, a sans serif by Jason Vandenberg designed to combine the warm feel of hand-written letters with the legibility of a clean sans serif. The book was printed on FSC™-certified 98gsm Yunshidai Ivory paper and bound in China.

Production was supervised by Leslie Cohen and Freesia Blizard
Book jacket and interiors designed by Chad Beckerman
Edited by Nick Thomas

LEVINE QUERIDO